JENNIFER LI SHOTZ

#1 *New York Times* bestselling author

HARPER
An Imprint of HarperCollinsPublishers

Scout: National Hero
Copyright © 2018 by Alloy Entertainment

alloyentertainment
Produced by Alloy Entertainment
1325 Avenue of the Americas
New York, NY 10019

Library of Congress Control Number: 2018933324
ISBN 978-0-06-280247-7 (paperback)
ISBN 978-0-06-280248-4 (hardcover)
ISBN 978-0-06-285728-6 (paper-over-board)

18 19 20 21 22 BRR 10 9 8 7 6 5 4 3
❖
First Edition

For all the helpers everywhere—
on two legs or four. Thank you.

1

MATT DIPPED THE LONG KAYAK PADDLE into the water of the Truckee River and angled it backward, just like his dad had taught him. He felt the familiar resistance as the kayak cut smoothly through the water.

He turned his head to the side and gazed up at the tall rocks that lined the river's canyon. The stone glowed red and gold in the afternoon sunlight. Matt decided this was the perfect way to spend his twelfth birthday—alone, with just the scrubby trees along the banks, the cool river beneath him, and the warm sun above.

He put his feet up on the seat in front of him and lay back, gazing at the cloudless blue sky. The weather was hot for early spring—even for Nevada. Matt had only lived in Silver Valley, a town about twenty minutes east of Reno, for a little over a month, but he already knew he wasn't supposed to be in a T-shirt and shorts at this time of year. Even his mom and older sister said that it was crazy warm. He'd heard on the news that there had been a lot of snow this past winter, and now with the superhot weather, the extra snow was melting faster than usual.

As Matt drifted along on the Truckee, he decided that Nevada was weird but beautiful. He had expected a desert, but there were huge, tall rock formations that looked like they belonged on Mars. He'd expected cactuses, but there were gnarled trees and flowering shrubs. He thought it would be dry, but there was not only the Truckee River but also tons of watering holes and reservoirs all over the place.

Today was the first day Matt had gotten a chance to take his kayak out on the river. His dad had only been in Silver Valley with them for a few days before he was deployed back to Afghanistan, but before he left he'd helped Matt build a bike trailer so he could get to the river by himself.

Matt knew he looked sort of ridiculous, pedaling awkwardly and dragging a thirteen-foot kayak behind him, but he didn't care. This was worth it. Plus it wasn't like he was going to run into anyone he knew. Matt wasn't on a first-name basis with any of the kids at his new school yet, even after all these weeks.

He knew he would get around to making friends eventually. But right now, he didn't see much point in trying. If he made friends, he'd probably just have to leave them soon anyway.

Besides, hanging by himself was a lot more fun—or maybe just a lot easier.

Matt felt the strong current of the swollen Truckee beneath him, tugging the kayak along. He barely needed to paddle. The kayak was a narrow, rigid three-seater with a molded top to sit on. He had plenty of room to stretch out and relax—and just float downstream without trying to steer.

There was one important rule Matt's dad had repeated a million times when they first started kayaking together: *Don't fight the water; work with it.* He meant that you had to be flexible, pay attention to what the water was doing, and save your energy for the right move.

Matt's phone chirped in his pocket. He ignored it. It chirped again. Then again.

With a groan, Matt pulled it out and squinted at the screen in the bright sunlight. There were four texts from his mom and one from his sister.

Where are you?

We're waiting for you.

Please come home now.

Mom is going to kill you if you don't get home now.

On my way, Matt texted back.

Another rule his dad had drilled into him before he left: *Don't ignore your mother's texts.*

By Matt's count, he and his family had lived in nine states in his twelve years on Earth. Both of his parents were in the military, but this recent move was for his mom's job, commanding an Army National Guard base. Who knew how long they'd be here.

His phone dinged again. He couldn't help but grin. His family knew him well.

You said you were leaving.

Matt paddled the kayak to the riverbank and hopped off sideways before it even came to a stop. He dragged the boat up onto the shore and took one last look at the shimmering river before heading home.

* * *

"Happy birthday, sweetheart!"

"Happy happy, little brother."

His mom and sister wrapped him in enthusiastic hugs. Behind them, his dad's face filled the computer screen.

"Happy birthday, buddy!" His voice was deep and familiar, even through the laptop speakers. He sounded a lot closer than 8,000 miles away. Matt waved at him, and his dad waved back.

Matt and Bridget both had their dad's straight, dark brown hair—though Matt wore his a little shaggy instead of in a crew cut, like his dad. Both kids had their mom's lanky frame instead of their dad's barrel-chested stockiness. But Matt had gotten his dad's piercing blue eyes, which Bridget constantly told him she should have gotten instead of him.

At the moment, the blue eyes on the computer screen looked red-rimmed, with dark circles underneath. Matt's dad was in his fatigues, and he hadn't shaved in a day or two. Matt guessed that he must have just come back from patrol.

"What time is it there?" Matt asked, walking over to the laptop.

His dad checked his watch. "Oh one hundred hours."

"Oof. Sorry to keep you up, Dad."

His dad grinned. "I wouldn't miss this, Matt-o!"

"Blow out the candles, honey," his mom said, leading him toward the kitchen island.

Matt's birthday cake was tilting sharply to one side. He'd just opened his mouth to make a joke about his sister's baking skills when she elbowed him in the ribs.

"Don't say a word." Bridget shot him serious side-eye. At seventeen, she could silence him with one look, even though she and Matt were almost the same height now. He'd already grown an inch in the weeks since they'd arrived in Nevada.

"Save me a piece of that cake, would you, Matt?" his dad said through the computer.

"Shouldn't be a problem," Matt said, poking at it with the tip of a knife. "It looks like it's carbonized already." He turned to Bridget. "Uh, I mean—sure, the cake is uh-maaaazing."

"You're so welcome," Bridget said. "Oh wait—you didn't actually say thank you, though, did you?"

"Thank you." Matt put down the knife and punched her lightly in the shoulder. She pinched him in return. "Really, thanks, guys." He meant it this time. "This is awesome."

"You're welcome, honey." His mom squeezed his shoulders and planted a kiss on the top of his head. She cut the cake, handed them hefty slices, and took one for herself. "Let's open some presents, shall we?" she mumbled through a mouthful.

His sister handed him a flat package. Matt unwrapped it quickly; it was a new video game that he'd been wanting.

"Sweet!" he said. "Thanks, Bridge."

"You're welcome, Stinker."

Matt's mom disappeared into another room and Bridget followed. They were in temporary housing, living on the base until they found their own place nearby—although as far as Matt could tell, no one had time to look at real estate. His dad certainly couldn't do it from the Middle East, and his mom was working at her new job pretty much around the clock.

Not only was Matt's mom running the whole National Guard base, she was also in charge of setting up a new National Guard K-9 unit. It was the first of its kind out west, and it was a big deal. His mom, Colonel Tackett, couldn't mess it up.

Matt had been shocked when his mom sat him down right before Christmas and told him they were moving in January. Her new position had come up quickly. Matt was used to moving, but this time he'd barely had time to say good-bye to his friends in Oregon.

And to make it even more stressful, Matt's dad was only halfway through a long deployment. He'd been able to take a few days' leave to help them move, but he wouldn't be home again for months, until he'd completed his mission.

Matt picked up the laptop and carried it over to the couch. He flopped down onto the cushions and propped the computer up on his knees.

"You still awake, Dad?"

"Yep." His dad yawned. "I can't believe you're twelve, my man."

Matt shrugged. "Yeah."

"You liking Nevada?"

Matt thought about it for a second. Nevada wasn't any worse than Tennessee or Ohio. And it wasn't quite as cool as Oregon. "Yeah," he was happy to say. "It's pretty awesome, actually. I took my kayak out on the river today."

"Glad to hear it," his dad said. "Because if you didn't like it, you were going to have to come live with me in the *real* desert here."

"Very funny."

His dad's voice got serious. "I know this was a tough move, Matt. I'm proud of how you've handled it."

"Thanks, Dad."

"'Cause what do we Tacketts do when we move to a new place?" His dad pointed into the camera at Matt, waiting for the response.

Matt rolled his eyes. He and Bridget had been hearing this one their whole lives. "We go all in," he mumbled.

"I'm sorry, I couldn't hear you, soldier. All in to what?" his dad prodded him, a huge grin on his face.

"All in to settle in," Matt responded, loudly and clearly. His dad had a full library of expressions and sayings that Matt knew by heart—and sometimes he enjoyed tormenting Matt with them.

"That's right. All in to settle in!"

Matt's mom and sister walked in carrying a long, thin package wrapped in festive birthday paper.

"Is he giving you the 'All in' speech again, Matt?" Bridget asked. "Totally unexpected, Dad."

"Oh shush, Bridge," their dad said. "Now let's open that present."

Matt knew what it was right away. He ripped off

the paper while his dad watched, an excited smile on his face.

It was the new fly-fishing rod and reel that Matt had wanted for months—the perfect equipment for catching trout. Fishing season didn't start till later in the year, but that gave Matt plenty of time to practice with his new gear.

"Thanks, Dad! Thanks, Mom!" Matt turned the rod over in his hands, admiring its light weight and cork handle. "It's so cool."

"You're welcome, pal." His dad's voice grew softer. "I can't wait to break it in with you. Promise you'll save me some fish?"

"Sure," Matt replied. "I'll save you some. Not a lot, but some."

"Uh, guys," Matt's mom interrupted. She was looking down at her phone. "Hate to break up the party, but I've got a situation."

"Copy that," Matt's dad said. "Love you guys."

"Love you!" they said in unison. Matt clicked off the call.

"What's up, Mom?" Bridget asked.

"Nothing bad. There's a new K-9 recruit coming in. The dog was supposed to get here tomorrow, but it looks like they put him on a plane a day early. Paperwork mix-up or something." She rubbed her temples, then looked at her watch. "If it wasn't the weekend I'd ask someone else to grab him, but it'll only take a minute to get to the airport anyway. Then we'll keep celebrating. Okay, Matt?"

"Sure."

"Guys, I have to go study," Bridget said.

"I'll come to the airport with you, Mom," Matt offered.

"Thanks, bud." His mom smiled at him. "You're the best."

"Yeah, yeah," Matt teased her. "I know. I'm the best."

2

"SO WHERE'D THIS DOG COME FROM?" Matt asked his mom as they drove to the airport.

"Remember Janine Perillo? We were in basic training together?"

"Yeah."

"She's a cop now—a K-9 officer in Mississippi. I'm taking the dog on her recommendation. Janine said this guy's got something special."

"What's his name?"

"Scout."

"Scout," Matt repeated. "That's a good name for a National Guard dog."

His mom nodded in agreement. "I told Janine I

need the best dogs in the country for my unit," she went on. "She said Scout grew up with the finest search-and-rescue dog she's ever known—a black Lab named Hero. He's a legend. Anyway, Janine said Scout has the same skills."

"Wow." Matt yawned. "Can't wait to meet this gifted pup."

"Well, I hope he's as good as she says." There was a worried note in her voice. "I need all the help I can get."

Traffic was light, and they got to the airport quickly. His mom followed signs to cargo pickup and flashed her badge at an officer. The man waved them through, and they pulled up outside a low building. A bored-looking clerk sat behind a single desk inside. After a bit of paperwork, he shuffled into the back of the building and returned pushing a flatbed dolly. On it was a large crate made of thick plastic, with a metal gate for a door and a row of air holes around the sides. The man rolled the dolly to a stop, heaved the crate onto the floor, turned around, and pushed the dolly into the back room again.

Matt couldn't see the whole dog inside—he could only see the tip of a tan-and-white snout with a black nose pressing through an air hole. A steady sound emanated from the crate—the sound of teeth on hard plastic.

Matt bent down to look. The dog was chewing on the inside of the crate, he realized. Every few minutes, Scout stopped gnawing, stuffed a paw through the opening, and scratched at it. Was he trying to widen it?

Scout wasn't freaking out, and he wasn't upset—he was just methodically trying to escape. Matt was immediately impressed.

Matt had never had his own dog before. They'd moved around too much for his family to have a pet of their own, but he'd spent enough time with his mom's K-9 units to know that this dog was smart.

Matt's mom crouched down beside the crate. "Hey, buddy," she said softly. "Hi, Scout."

The chewing stopped for a second. Matt dropped to his knees by his mom's side and peered through the metal bars of the door with her.

There, staring back at him, was a giant pair of eyes: dark brown, rounded, and full of intensity. They locked on Matt, and Matt couldn't look away. He felt as if Scout was trying to communicate—as if he was saying *I don't know where I am or who you are, but I'm going to figure it out.*

Surrounding the eyes was a handsome face: thick, soft brown fur streaked with white and a white snout, topped off with two tall, pointy ears that each seemed to have a mind of its own. One ear aimed straight up to the sky, while the other spun forward and pointed right at Matt. Matt couldn't tell what kind of dog Scout was, but he looked like some sort of mix.

Scout's ears danced around on his head. It was as if he was listening to everything all at once—to Matt and his mom, to the airplanes taxiing just outside, to the clamor of truck doors opening and closing. Clearly this dog didn't miss a beat.

Nor did he miss a scent. Scout sniffed at Matt and his mom through the grate and at the air around him. He sniffed at Matt's outstretched hand and the knee of his jeans right outside the crate's door. Matt wondered what Scout could smell that he couldn't.

"Hi, Scout," Matt said softly. He leaned forward until his face was close to Scout's black nose. They were about the same height when Matt was kneeling, which meant Scout was already pretty big for a one-year-old dog. Scout sniffed Matt's face through the bars and snorted a couple of times to clear his nostrils.

Matt stuck his fingers through the bars of the door,

and Scout pressed his cold, wet nose into them. He paused for a second, then licked Matt's knuckles once, twice. Then, without warning, he began pacing back and forth and scratching at the crate's door.

Matt looked up at his mom. "He's a good dog."

Matt's mom screwed up her mouth and watched Scout, studying him. "He does seem like a good dog," she agreed. "But there's something else going on too. He's a little . . . I don't know." She shook her head. "There's something about him I can't put my finger on. It's almost like he's . . . alert. Hyperalert. He might be too . . . I don't know . . . too clever for us. He's got to be obedient to be a good search-and-rescue dog."

Matt knew the look on her face. He could tell that her brain was whirring, running down the list of possible options and outcomes. She was a decisive person. Matt knew that if she didn't think Scout could cut it, the dog wouldn't get a second chance.

"Give him some time, Mom," he said. "He just got off a plane—he's probably just a little overwhelmed."

She looked doubtful. "Well, we'll have to wait and see. But maybe it's a good thing that they're not ready for him at the training center yet. I don't want to throw him right into the mix too quickly. We should bring him home with us for a couple of days. Just to get him settled."

Matt's mom was a dog expert. She'd grown up training them on her parents' farm, and she had worked in K-9 units her entire career. And she *knew* dogs—she understood them. He had never known her to be wrong about one before.

But for some reason, Matt didn't think she was right about Scout.

"What's that?" she asked, pointing to a crumpled envelope clipped to the crate. Matt reached for it and pulled out a handwritten note.

"That's weird," his mom said. "What does it say?"

Matt read the neat, scratchy handwriting out loud.

Dear Lucky New Owner of My Dog Scout,

You now have the best dog in the world. I've known Scout since he was a goofy puppy. But Scout was trained by Hero, the best search-and-rescue dog IN THE WORLD, and now Scout is a great search-and-rescue dog too. Scout and Hero saved me and my friends a few times. He's super smart and I want him to have a really cool job and save lots of lives.

Please take good care of him and tell him I said hi.

—Jack Murphy

P.S. I'll always miss Scout, but don't worry, now I have a new puppy.

"Whoa," Matt said. "Sounds like Scout's already a hero."

"It sure does," Matt's mom said. "But we'll have to see for ourselves what he's got."

Matt and his mom lifted Scout's crate into the back of their SUV. The dog chewed on the plastic the whole drive home. He didn't seem to care that he was in a car. He didn't seem too concerned with where he was being taken. He just kept at it.

Matt looked back from the passenger seat, but all he could see was Scout's fur poking through the openings in the side of the crate. He looked at his mom's face to see what she was thinking, but she just stared straight ahead through the windshield, her jaw tight.

They got Scout back to base and, together, hauled

the heavy crate into the house, setting it up in a corner of the kitchen. Matt leaned against the kitchen counter, and Scout watched him through the metal bars.

"Matt, I have to run over to the office to deal with Scout's paperwork. I need you to stay with him."

"Sure, Mom."

Matt got up, crossed the kitchen, and filled a bowl with water while Scout followed him with his eyes. Matt set the bowl down just outside the crate. He slid the latch to the side and swung open the door, then scooted out of the way.

The dog stopped gnawing. He looked out the open door—and sat down.

There was nothing stopping Scout from escaping his enclosure, but he didn't move. Matt knew dogs were den animals and they felt safe in their crates, but usually they were happy to get out and stretch their legs after being cooped up for a long time.

Matt and Scout stared at each other through the opening. Matt stayed very still, not wanting to spook the dog.

After a couple of moments, Scout rose to a low crouch and sniffed at the air. He took a small step forward and stuck his nose out of the crate. With his ears pressed back against the sides of his head, he looked around cautiously.

Matt wanted to reach out and pet the dog, to make him feel comfortable, but he needed to give Scout some space.

Matt waited.

Scout sat back down and fixed Matt with that piercing gaze again. A strange thought occurred to Matt. This wasn't his dog, and Scout certainly didn't have any reason to think Matt was the head of the pack. But Scout looked like he was waiting for something . . . Could it be a command?

It was worth a shot.

"Scout," Matt said, "you can get up."

Scout just stared at him.

"Um, Scout, get up?"

Nothing. But Scout's face was a little more animated— Matt was on the right track. He just needed to figure out the right word.

"Scout—okay!"

That was it.

Scout hopped to his feet. He extended one paw out of the crate and put it down on the kitchen floor. Then the next. His fuzzy white-and-brown head followed. He stood for a moment, partly out of the crate, partly in it. He held himself perfectly still, his muscles tensed and his tail straight out behind him. Only his head moved as he surveyed the room, taking in the birthday cake left on the counter, the floodlights on the base streaming in through the window, the gleaming floors.

Matt sat down on the floor a few feet away and tried not to move much. It was the first time he'd seen all of Scout. He was bigger than Matt had realized—taller and sturdier. His legs were long and lean, but muscular, and his chest was solid. Scout was a strong, handsome dog, but there was also a watchfulness to him—a quickness—which told Matt that Scout was more than just brawn. This dog was clearly full of brains too.

Scout turned to look at Matt and tipped his head to the side, studying Matt's face. He stepped toward Matt, his nails clacking on the kitchen floor, until his snout was right in Matt's face. Matt tried not to blink as Scout sniffed at his hair and cheeks, his ears and eye sockets. He stifled a laugh as Scout exhaled sharply into his eyebrow.

The dog turned away from Matt and began to move around the kitchen. Scout's ears pricked up at the distant sound of a truck starting. When the dish-washer hummed and vibrated, his head shot around. He sniffed at the floor along the cabinets and licked up a couple of cake crumbs. Matt hopped to his feet and followed Scout as he made his way into the living room. After a thorough investigation of the couch, beanbag chair, and television cabinet, Scout made his way up the stairs.

Matt followed Scout down the hall as the dog moved steadily along—almost as if he knew exactly where he was going. Scout sniffed at Matt's parents' doorway, then his sister's, but he didn't stop until he reached Matt's room. He nosed the half-closed door open and stepped inside. With barely a look around, Scout trotted across the room and hopped up onto Matt's bed.

There was a pile of dirty clothes on the bed that Matt had meant to take downstairs. Scout sniffed at the clothes, then nudged them onto the floor with his head.

"Make yourself at home!" Matt laughed.

Scout blinked at Matt, then with a glance around the room at Matt's fishing gear and new fishing pole, old kayak paddle, camping lantern, and stacks of books,

Scout lay down, dropped his head onto his paws, and let out a long exhale.

Matt sat down on the bed and held out a hand toward Scout's neck. Scout didn't pull away, so Matt ran his fingers through Scout's fur—it was even thicker than he had expected. He scratched beneath Scout's collar, and Scout closed his eyes. When Matt stopped, Scout opened his eyes and looked up at him. The dog sat up, licked Matt's face once, and dropped back down, resting his head on Matt's knee.

In no time, Scout had gone from being anxious in his crate to acting like he'd lived with this family forever. Matt tried to figure out why the dog's behavior had changed so much so fast. Maybe it was because it was just the two of them and the house was quiet. Or maybe he reminded Scout of his old owner, Jack.

Whatever the reason, it was clear to Matt that Scout liked him.

Matt grinned from ear to ear. He gently scratched Scout's ears and smoothed the soft fur on his head.

They sat like that for a few minutes. Matt listened to the sounds of the base outside—men and women training, trucks rolling by, soldiers laughing as they walked together.

"Now what, Scout?" he asked.

Matt didn't really know what to do with a dog. Did the dog just go wherever you went? Was there something he was supposed to be doing for Scout?

Matt eyed the fishing rod leaning in the corner and had an idea. He eased his leg out from under the dog's head.

"Stay here," he said. Scout stayed.

Matt ran downstairs and came back up in a flash. He put a plate of cold cuts down on his dresser, and the smell of the food instantly got Scout's attention. His head popped up and his nose twitched like crazy as he hopped off the bed and ran over to Matt. He sat down at Matt's feet, an eager, impatient look in his eye.

"Patience, Scout," Matt said. Matt connected the reel to the rod and knotted the line in all the right places. Then he wound the line onto the reel and threaded it through the guides—but he left off the hook. Scout's ears flicked at the whirring and clicking sounds.

Matt looked down at Scout. "You ready?" he asked. Scout's ears and brow shot up simultaneously. Matt ripped off a small piece of ham and gently knotted the end of the fishing line around it. He raised the rod, and the ham hung in the air above their heads.

Scout studied the dangling lunch meat, confused. He tipped his head at an angle, and his eyes scrunched together in the middle of his forehead.

"Here it comes," Matt said. And with a smooth motion in the small room, he raised the rod over his shoulder, then angled it forward, releasing the line at the same time. The ham arced through the air, flying out over the bed until Matt stopped the line with his finger and brought the meat's trajectory to a sudden halt.

Scout was back on the bed in a flash, looking straight up at the food bobbing over his head. His snout was working overtime. After a couple of fruitless swipes in the air with a paw, Scout sat down and slowly raised himself up on his hind legs, until he was sitting back on his haunches with his front paws in the air.

With a lightning-quick movement, Scout snatched the ham and scarfed it down. Then he lowered himself back down onto the bed and fixed his gaze on the end of the fishing line, waiting for more.

Matt reloaded and cast the meat toward his desk this time. Scout bounded off the bed and up onto Matt's desk chair so quickly that Matt laughed out loud.

"You're seriously fast, Scout."

They went on like this until Bridget stuck her head in the door.

"Sounds like fun in here," she said.

"Watch this," Matt said. He loaded up a piece of ham and held the rod over his shoulder, ready to cast. But Scout wasn't in position, ready to go after it. He was . . . done. The dog had wandered over to Bridget and was sniffing at her feet, then her knees.

"Awwwww!" she exclaimed. "You're so cute!" She dropped to the floor, and Scout sniffed at her hair while she gave him a good scratch.

After a few minutes, Bridget tore herself away from Scout and went back to her room to study. Scout followed her to the door and watched her leave.

Matt dropped down on the floor by his bed. Scout walked back to him, spun around in a circle three times, and plopped down by Matt's side, his tags jingling as he put his head down on his paws. Matt put his arm around Scout's neck.

Scout had only been in Nevada for a couple of hours, but he already seemed right at home.

"I guess we're both the new kid," Matt said to the dog. "But like my dad always says, 'all in to settle in.'"

3

MATT SPENT THE NEXT DAY AT school daydreaming about fun games to play with Scout. As soon as the second bell rang, he raced down the steps to the carpool line. He was eager to get home and see the dog.

As he stood waiting for his mom, Matt heard a loud burst of laughter from behind him. He looked over his shoulder, back toward the two-story stone building. A small group of girls and boys gathered around the bike rack, unlocking their bikes. A couple of them waved at Matt, but a few others just gave him the look. He could practically see the thought bubbles above their heads: *Where's he from? Is he cool? Why did he move here?*

Matt was used to the stares every time he started at a new school, but that didn't mean he liked being gawked at like a space alien. *I'm not a Martian,* he wanted to tell them.

Someone brushed against Matt's arm, and he spun around to see a tall, skinny kid with brown skin, short black hair, and glasses. Matt recognized him from math class, and maybe English—or was it PE? It was hard to keep track of all the new faces in a new school . . . again.

"Sorry, man," the boy said distractedly. He was half on, half off his bike, wrestling with his heavy backpack. His phone started to slip out of his pocket, and his hand shot out to catch it at the last second.

"First day with the new glasses?" Matt blurted out before he could stop himself. He cringed. It was such a dorky joke—one he would have made to his friend Nico back in Oregon. But Nico knew Matt and got his sense of humor—and would have made an even cornier joke right back.

This boy, however, had no idea that Matt was just kidding. He shot Matt a confused look, his mouth angling into a semi-smile, like he was trying to figure out if the new kid was being purposefully funny or not.

"Uh, I guess so?" the boy replied before turning away and starting to push his bike.

Matt wanted to kick himself for being so lame. He watched the boy walk away and scrambled to think of something to say.

"You're in Ms. Chang's math class, right?" Matt called out. "Third period?"

The kid stopped and turned around. He nodded. "It's hard, right?"

"Yeah." Matt pulled a funny face. "And math is supposed to be my strongest subject."

Thankfully, the boy laughed.

"I'm Matt."

"I'm Dev." He held out his hand for a fist bump. Matt gave him a tap.

Behind Dev, a large black SUV stopped at the curb. It was Matt's mom.

The front passenger window rolled down, and Scout's head popped out. He barked once at Matt. Dev spun around at the sound.

Before Matt could call out to Scout, the dog propelled himself through the open window, landed lightly on the ground, and trotted over to Matt.

"Scout!" Matt's mom yelled. "Come!" But Scout

ignored her and jumped up on Matt with his front paws, his tail wagging like crazy. He stood way up on his back legs and stretched his snout toward Matt's face, excited to give him a lick hello.

"Hi, Scout," Matt said. He scratched him behind both ears. "Nice to see you too."

"Cool dog!" Dev reached over and patted Scout. "Seems like he missed you."

"I guess." Matt laughed. "But he's not my dog—not really."

"Well," Dev said, settling himself onto his bike, "he's still cool. See you in class tomorrow."

"See you," Matt said, placing Scout's front paws back on the ground and taking a firm hold of his collar.

Dev shot off on his bike, popped a wheelie, and was gone, leaving Matt impressed with his bike skills—and relieved that he hadn't made a total fool out of himself.

"Scout, come!" his mom called. Once again, Scout ignored her.

Matt opened the passenger door of the car. "Up, Scout." Scout followed Matt's command and hopped right in. Matt scooted him off the front seat, and the dog settled in the back.

Matt's mom rolled her eyes. "Seriously, Scout?" She sounded frustrated.

"Sorry, Mom. I guess he just listens to me."

"It's not your fault, pal." She steered the car out of the parking lot and onto the street. "But it's good timing that we're on our way to the training center. The K-9 unit is going to start working with him today. Hopefully he'll do a better job listening there."

"Can I come watch?" Matt asked. He wanted to see Scout get to work.

"Sure thing. Let's just hope that Scout listens to his new handlers better than he listens to me."

Once on base, Matt followed his mom through a small door in a massive, warehouse-size building. The building could have contained anything—a factory, a TV studio, a furniture store.

But inside was one of the most advanced K-9 training facilities in the world.

The facility had only recently been finished, and it was a dog's—and a dog handler's—dream come true.

There were big, comfortable kennels for the animals. There was a medical treatment space, a grooming area, and open training rings for handlers and dogs to practice commands. There were agility courses where dogs tiptoed up and down ladders, clambered over wobbly wooden platforms, scrambled across narrow beams, and wriggled through tunnels and tubes.

And best of all, there were mock disaster zones that simulated the kinds of emergency situations these K-9s—and soldiers—might find themselves in. A teetering pile of concrete rubble served as a collapsed building. A wasteland of splintered beams and shards of building materials re-created the wreckage of a tornado or hurricane. And outside, real buildings and cars were almost entirely submerged in water to simulate a flood zone.

Matt had heard his mom talk about the facility so many times he could practically recite her words himself. The National Guard could be called into service for any kind of emergency, from natural disasters in their region to battle in a foreign country. They had to be prepared for any possibility, and so did the dogs. At this facility, they trained dogs for different kinds of search and rescue: disaster search, trailing and tracking, water recovery, air scenting, and even cadaver detection.

Scout was supposed to be a great trailing or tracking dog.

But that was going to be put to the test today.

Matt thought Scout had a lot of the qualities a good search-and-rescue dog needed. He was extra alert, and he was definitely strong and quick. He had a sweet temperament and liked people.

But Scout also seemed . . . different. For one thing, most search-and-rescue dogs had big personalities— they were goofy and happy, and active to the point of being hyper. When they found a favorite toy, they became completely obsessed with it. The perfect combination was an energetic dog who would chase the same toy again and again—who, in fact, was almost impossible to distract from that toy.

It was called having a "high drive." High drive was what made a rescue dog keep going until it found what it was after, whether that was a toy, a treat, or a person in need of rescuing.

Scout, on the other hand, had a great time fishing for cold cuts in Matt's room, but lost interest when Bridget came in. Did that mean he wouldn't have the focus to stay on the trail of a lost kid?

High drive made K-9 dogs great at their jobs . . . but

it also made them exhausting to have around the house if they weren't well trained. At least that's how Matt's mom had explained the Fern incident.

When Matt was little, one of his mom's work dogs, Fern, had been staying at their house and decided that Matt's stuffed koala was her absolute most favorite toy. Fern snatched up the bear and wouldn't let it go for anything. Every time Matt's mom managed to get it away from her—while Matt sobbed nearby—a very excited Fern thought they were playing a training game. His parents would hide the bear, and Fern would go nuts and hunt it down again. She found the koala in the back of Matt's closet, in the laundry room, and at the top of a kitchen cabinet.

Needless to say, Fern was not invited back to the house. But she made an excellent search-and-rescue dog.

Matt's mom handed Scout's leash to a dog handler.

"He's all yours, Sergeant Klein," she said.

"Can't wait, Colonel," Klein said. He unclipped the leash and gave Scout a couple of minutes to sniff out his new surroundings. Scout followed his nose around the training ring. There were several other dogs at work, most of them younger than Scout—and most of them much more energetic and playful.

Klein studied Scout carefully and made some notes on a clipboard.

Across the cavernous space, another handler held out a baseball cap to a large German shepherd at her feet. The dog buried her nose in it, sniffing it all over. After a moment, the handler took it away.

With the exception of Fern, Matt had always loved watching dogs search for scent objects. He moved closer so he could watch the shepherd at work.

"Stay," the handler said firmly.

The dog sat still as a statue while the woman climbed onto a pile of rubble. She came back down a moment later empty-handed.

"Search!" the handler said. The dog zipped up onto the pile, searching for the hat, moving quickly but purposefully up, over, and around the rough and uneven surface. The shepherd was full of energy, almost playful, like the search was one big game. The dog's snout grazed the concrete and bobbed in the air. Her tail shot straight up like an antenna.

Then all of a sudden, she froze in her tracks, sat down, and barked.

The handler climbed over, fed the dog a treat, and praised her, then bent down and pulled the cap out from under a leaning chunk of concrete. The dog wagged her tail, pleased with herself.

"Scout, sit," Matt heard Sergeant Klein say behind him. Matt came back to watch them at work. Scout sat. "Stay," Klein said. He walked a few feet away, testing Scout's mastery of a basic command.

Scout stayed, but just barely. His ears perked up and rotated back; Matt could tell that he was getting distracted. A couple of dogs exchanged barks at the far side of the room. Scout turned his head toward the sound and rose partway up on his haunches, as if he were thinking about running over to them.

Klein made a few notes on his clipboard. Matt tried to see what the sergeant was seeing in Scout. He was relieved when Scout sat all the way down again and waited patiently.

"What do you think?" Klein came up beside Matt. They stood side by side, watching as Scout waited to be released from the *stay* command.

Matt thought for a moment before replying. "I think he's really smart. And he knows the rules, but it's like he . . . focuses on everything at once instead of just one thing."

"I'm Scott Klein." The handler extended a hand. "You're the colonel's son?"

"Yes, sir. I'm Matt." He took Klein's hand and gripped it firmly, like his parents had always taught him.

"I think you might be right about Scout. He's smart, he's got skills, but he's a little jumpy. I'm just not sure yet whether it's the new environment or the big move, but let's hope he can settle down a bit."

Scout was starting to get antsy. He raised a paw and swiped at the ground, then ducked his head down and up again, as if he was testing to see just how much he could get away with.

"You want to give it a try?" Klein asked.

Matt hesitated. He had never trained a dog before, but over the years, he had watched his mom patiently run dozens of dogs through the same commands over and over.

"I hear Scout really responds to you," Klein said. "Maybe you can help us figure him out."

"Sure." Matt shrugged. "Why not?"

Klein dropped a handful of treats into Matt's hand. "Go for it."

Matt stepped toward Scout. Scout wagged his tail, as if to say "Finally!" But he stayed seated.

As Matt inched closer, Scout simply couldn't contain himself anymore. He hopped up and wagged his tail so hard the whole back half of his body swished back and forth.

"Hey, buddy," Matt said. "Sit."

Scout looked confused. His tail stopped and his body went still. He tilted his head to the side and crinkled up his brow. Matt knew he wasn't supposed to repeat the command right away—he needed to give Scout a moment to respond. If you repeated it too many times, it would lose its meaning to the dog. Plus you had to teach them to respond the first time.

Matt waited. When Scout finally realized that nothing else was going to happen until he sat, he sat.

"Good dog," Matt said. He gave Scout a treat. Matt looked away from Scout, testing to see if the dog would stay seated. Scout watched Matt intently but didn't move. Matt took a step backward. Scout stayed put. Matt walked a few feet away and turned his back to Scout. He heard a quiet woof rise in the dog's throat—but he could tell that Scout still hadn't moved.

Matt turned around to face the dog. Scout watched him earnestly, impatiently.

"Okay!" Matt said. With that command, Scout knew he was free to move. He leaped to his feet and happily walked and wagged his way to Matt's side. "Sit," Matt said. Scout sat. Matt gave him a treat.

They went on like this for some time, with Matt running through a few more simple commands.

"Okay," Klein said, "stop giving him treats now and see what happens."

Without the instant payoff, Scout's accuracy dropped to about 50 percent. Scout got distracted, or sat but hopped right up again, or crouched instead of lying all the way down. When he did get it right, though, Scout really nailed it. His response time was amazing and his movements were precise—but, Matt could see, only when the dog *wanted* them to be.

Matt was starting to understand that Scout was perfectly capable of being a top-notch search-and-rescue dog. He just had to want it.

Scout had been trained for far more than *sit*, *down*, *come*, and *stop*. But Matt didn't know how to give the more complicated commands, like *search* or *show me*. He had never actually been on a search mission with a dog, or watched a handler at work in the field.

"Try something a little harder with him," Klein suggested. "Like, how about a *go out* command."

"You mean the one where I tell him to walk ahead of me and stop?" Matt asked.

"That's the one. Just be sure to say it with conviction. If you don't buy it, Scout won't either."

Matt wasn't sure he knew what that meant, but he was willing to give it a try. "So I just say 'go out'?"

"That's it," Klein said. "Pick the spot you want him to walk to. Point toward it, and keep your eye on it as he heads over. And then when he's just a step away from that spot, tell him to stop. If he's as good as they say he is, he should stop before he puts the next paw down."

"Wow." Matt shook his head. "That's crazy."

"Some of the best working dogs out there—I've heard their handlers say it was like the dog knew where they were supposed to stop before they even got the command. And they can also do it with just a hand signal, by the way."

"No way," Matt said. "Can Scout do all that?"

"That's what we're going to find out." Klein grinned at him. "Go for it. Use your hand signals."

Matt turned to the dog.

"Scout," Matt said, lowering his voice and trying to sound serious. "Go out." He pointed toward the wall. Scout eyed him suspiciously. Matt waited. He looked at Klein for direction. Klein nodded, encouraging him. Matt cleared his throat and said it again. "Go out!"

Scout hopped to his feet and stepped in the direction Matt was pointing, and suddenly, he was like a different dog. He was focused and in total control of his body. He moved gracefully, stealthily, like a predator stepping toward its prey. He did not hop around happily like the other dogs in the ring.

Matt waited until Scout was a few feet from the wall. "Stop," he said. Scout stopped short, as if someone had flipped the off switch on his body. It wasn't quite instantaneous, but close. He sat down silently and turned to look back at Matt.

Matt's jaw dropped. "That was amazing, Scout!"

"Nice!" Klein said. He held up his hand for a high five, and Matt slapped it.

"You ready to go, Matt?" His mom walked up to the training area, staring down at the phone in her hand. She looked up and saw Matt and Klein standing together and Scout sitting across the ring. She smiled.

"You helping with Scout?"

Matt grinned. "Yeah. He's doing great, Mom!"

His mom gave Klein a questioning look. "What do you think? I'm not so sure this dog has what it takes."

The smile slipped from the sergeant's face. He pressed his lips together, shot a guilty sideways glance at Matt, and shook his head, like he hated delivering bad news. "He's inconsistent," Klein said. "He lacks focus and has a strong mind of his own."

Matt couldn't believe what he was hearing. Had they just been watching the same dog?

"I don't know, Mom," Matt blurted out. She and Klein stared at him. "Cut him some slack." Matt's cheeks started burning. There was something about Scout that he just . . . understood.

Matt held up his hands and searched for the right words. "Scout's the new guy. Sometimes that's not easy."

4

IN MATT'S EXPERIENCE, THERE WERE TWO kinds of PE teachers in the world: those who were overly enthusiastic, and those who were grumpy and mean, as if they were always having a bad day.

Unfortunately for Matt, his new gym teacher was the grumpy type.

Matt was lucky; he was a good runner and could shoot a basket. But that didn't mean he enjoyed PE. He had never had the patience for organized sports. He was much happier outside, on his own or with his dad—kayaking, mountain biking, or fishing.

But there'd been one good surprise at this new school: The gym had a rock-climbing wall.

The climbing wall consisted of floor-to-ceiling panels covered in dozens of colorful plastic holds. The trick was to hang on to the holds with your fingertips and toes—and nothing else—and make your way to the very top.

Matt had never gone rock climbing before, and he'd always wanted to try it.

But one thing he *hadn't* wanted? To try climbing for the first time ever in front of his entire PE class at his brand-new school.

Matt stood at the front of the line; he was up next. He stretched out his fingers and bobbed up and down on his toes anxiously. A couple of boys elbowed one another playfully right behind him. It was last period, and everyone was ready for school to be over.

When the teacher blew the whistle, Matt ran for the wall, clipped into his belay—the harness-and-rope system that made sure he wouldn't fall—hopped onto the lowest holds, and started reciting the safety check that their PE teacher had drilled into them before letting them get within five feet of the wall.

"On belay," Matt said.

"Belay on," his teacher replied.

"Ready to climb," Matt said.

"Climb away," his teacher finished.

And Matt began to climb.

He'd been carefully studying the kids ahead of him, observing their hand placement and how they pushed off with their toes. How hard could it be? Matt thought.

The answer came quickly: very hard. Way harder than it looked.

The holds seemed a lot smaller up close. Matt fumbled around with his fingers and toes, grasping for the holds that would give him the greatest leverage to push higher on his next move.

He thought about Scout as he climbed—the way the dog had used his whole body in training yesterday. Every single part of Scout was alert. Matt wanted to be like that too.

Matt kept making his way upward. And then he heard a surprising sound: his classmates chanting his name.

"Matt! Matt! Matt! Gooooo, Matt!"

He had no idea they even knew his name.

And why were they *cheering*?

That's when Matt looked up and discovered that he

was already three-quarters of the way to the top of the wall. It felt like he had just started climbing. How had he gotten there so fast?

His concentration broken, Matt suddenly became aware of the fact that he was fifteen feet off the ground. The holds beneath his fingers felt even smaller, and they were getting slippery from the sweat on his palms. His left leg began to shake from exertion, and he felt the weight of all those stares on his back.

He was starting to lose his nerve.

Matt took a deep breath and tried to focus.

"You good, Matt?" his teacher called out from below.

"Yep," Matt shouted down, his voice a little shaky.

"Why don't you come on down now?"

Matt exhaled. He was just a few feet from the top—and he wanted to get there. But he also knew what his dad had always taught him: *If something doesn't feel right, don't do it.* He wasn't exactly in danger here, but he didn't feel totally in control. He had lost his focus, and Matt didn't have any desire to fall off the wall in front of a gym full of kids with smartphones and social media accounts.

He let the teacher belay him down and unclip the

carabiner from his harness. Matt's cheeks burned with embarrassment as he turned to face his silent classmates.

He had failed.

Matt looked around the room, at the floor, over their heads—anywhere but at them. He steeled himself to walk to the locker room without looking anyone in the eye.

But Matt was totally wrong. He stole a glance and was surprised to see that the other kids were staring at him, their mouths hanging open in awe.

A tall boy pushed through to the front of the class—a boy Matt recognized.

"Matt!" Dev raised a hand in the air, and a huge grin spread across his face. "That was incredible!"

Matt felt a surge of embarrassment as he remembered his dorky joke to Dev the day before. He'd sounded so lame. But now Dev was clearly waiting for a high five.

Matt lifted his hand, and Dev slapped it with surprising force.

Matt ignored his stinging palm. "Thanks," he said with a shrug.

"So you climb?"

"That was my first time."

"No way!"

A group of boys and girls came up behind Dev. Matt recognized some of them from the cluster of kids by the bike rack the day before. His heart picked up speed. His hands were tingling from the climb. He shook out his fingers.

"Curtis, did you see that?" Dev asked the boy to his right.

Curtis bobbed his head in appreciation. "No one's gotten up that wall that fast." He gave Matt a fist bump. "Nicely done."

"Thanks." Matt exhaled.

"Hey, have you—" Dev was interrupted by the bell signaling the end of the school day. His classmates let out a whoop and headed for the locker room.

"Let's hit it, Dev," one of the girls said. She had long brown hair and freckles on her nose. "I want to get there before it gets packed."

"Coming, Amaiya," Dev said. Matt hoped Dev would finish the sentence he had started, but the boy turned toward the locker room and started to walk away.

Then Dev stopped and turned back. "You just moved here, right?" he asked Matt.

Matt nodded.

"You been to the ravine yet?"

Matt shook his head. He'd never even heard of it.

"It's like a half mile behind the school," Dev said. "There's a swimming hole and everyone jumps in from the rocks. There's some good bouldering there too. You should come with us."

"Sure," Matt said, not at all sure how he would convince his mom to let him go. "I just have to—" He stopped himself. These guys didn't need to know that he had to check with his mom first.

"No worries," Dev said. "If you can make it, just meet us out front in ten."

"Cool," Matt said.

"Cool," Dev said.

In the locker room, Matt threw on his shorts and T-shirt, balled up his gym clothes and jammed them into his backpack, then ran out a side door. He fished his phone out of his bag and quickly texted his mom. He knew there was only one reason she would let him go out on his own after school: new friends.

Ok if I hang out with some kids for a bit? Staying close to school.

His finger hesitated over the *send* button. He wasn't

lying exactly . . . he just wasn't telling her the whole truth. Right? He tapped the screen. The little whoosh sound was barely done when three little dots popped up, telling him that his mom was already typing a reply.

Of course! she wrote back. *Have fun! I'll pick you up at 4:30 in front of school?*

See you then. Thanks Mom.

Matt wasn't totally sure what he was doing—or even what the ravine was—but he wasn't going to over-think it. Just like Scout starting his K-9 training, Matt needed to dive in headfirst.

5

MATT STUFFED THE PHONE INTO HIS back pocket before his mom had a chance to change her mind. He headed around to the front of the building, where Dev and his friends had gathered. They were all hopping on their bikes.

Matt's heart sank. His mom had driven him to school that morning. He didn't have his bike.

Dev followed Matt's gaze to the bikes, all lined up in a row like dominoes. He seemed to get what Matt was thinking. "Go ahead, guys," Dev said to his friends. "Meet you there."

He turned back to Matt. "It's cool. I'll show you how to get there."

"Thanks," Matt said.

Dev pushed his bike and walked. He led Matt around the back of the school and cut through a stand of trees. They came out on a quiet, empty street lined with houses. Dev and Matt followed it for a few minutes until it dead-ended in a cul-de-sac.

Matt was confused—there was no ravine here—but Dev gestured to follow him down a narrow walkway between two houses. They came out into a wide-open, rust-and-sand-colored expanse of rocks, dirt, and shrub brush.

It was like they had suddenly left civilization behind and stumbled into an expansive desert.

They crunched over the uneven, dusty ground, Dev's bike bouncing along beside him. The afternoon sun warmed Matt's face. It was hot but not unbearable.

Matt had never been in this area before. He tried to pay careful attention, looking for any landmarks that would help him get back to school, in case he needed to get there on his own. He looked back over his shoulder at the last two houses he could see. He memorized their rooflines and the color of the curtains in the windows. He checked the position of the sun in relation to them, and did some quick calculations about which direction they were heading: west.

Matt had his mom and dad to thank for his ability to figure out his own location. When both your parents were in the military, you learned to navigate, no matter where you were—and no matter the circumstances.

"So, did you grow up in Silver Valley?" Matt asked as he and Dev walked along.

"Yep, my whole life," Dev said. "When did you move here?"

"Oh, uh . . ." Matt counted backward to the day they'd pulled up in the U-Haul to the base. "About five weeks."

"Dude, you're, like, brand-new."

"I guess so." Matt laughed.

"Moving sucks," Dev said with a shake of his head. "We moved houses when I was in fourth grade and I swear, my parents were stressed for a year."

Matt shrugged. "I'm used to it. We do it a lot."

"Military parents?"

"Yeah. We've moved nine times since I was born."

"Nine?"

"Nine."

"Man."

"Nevada seems cool."

Dev scanned the landscape around them like he was noticing it for the first time. "It's an okay place, I guess. Hot. But fun."

"Do you rock climb a lot?"

Dev nodded. "Since I was a little kid. My older sister taught me. She's really good."

"My sister definitely doesn't know how to rock climb." Matt laughed. "But my dad taught me to kayak when I was a kid. And fish. When he gets back we're going to find a good spot nearby and go fishing for a few days."

"Where is he?"

"Deployed."

Dev nodded. "My sister works on the base. She's a civilian. Is that where you live?"

"Yeah." Matt didn't tell Dev that his mom ran the base—which technically made her Dev's sister's boss.

A wide rock formation appeared in the distance, erupting from the ground and angling toward the sky. As they got closer, Matt saw that the solid mass was actually a series of craggy boulders that looked as if they'd been smashed together with great force. At the foot of these rocks was a pool of water, like an oasis.

The watering hole wasn't huge—it was maybe twenty feet across at its widest point—but it was enough to hold the group of kids who were splashing around in it. They shouted at one another loudly, and their laughter bounced off the stone face above them.

"This spot is awesome!" Matt said. In all the places he'd lived, all over the country, Matt had never seen anything as cool as this.

"*This spot*," Dev replied, "is the ravine."

Dev dropped his bike to the ground and led Matt along a path that wrapped up and around the boulders. The path got tricky fast. The boys had to pick their way around a series of smaller stones and pull themselves over chunky rocks to keep moving.

They rounded a curve and Matt saw that they had reached the top of the rock formation, about ten feet above the water's green surface. From up here, Matt could see the whole valley. The sky was clear and the town of Silver Valley was laid out in the distance, and beyond that were the Sierra Nevada mountains.

Dev let out a loud *whooooooop!* and kicked off his shoes, pulled off his T-shirt, and threw it on the ground before hurling himself—in his shorts—off the side of the boulder. He dropped straight down and sliced into the water feetfirst.

Matt felt his shoulders tense. He knew that he was next—and he'd never done anything like this before. He looked down from above. The water was so deep he couldn't see the bottom.

The other kids let out a cheer as Dev came up for air.

"Come on!" Dev called up to Matt from below.

Matt's heart skipped a beat, but he took off his shoes and set them aside. He pulled off his shirt and thanked his lucky stars he'd worn shorts to school.

Matt walked to the edge and gripped the rock with his toes, getting a feel for the surface.

"Do it, Matt!" some of the other kids in the water started yelling. "You can do it!"

Matt bent his knees, thrust himself upward and outward, and leaped. He felt himself falling straight down, like a bullet, piercing the surface and plunging toward the center of the earth. Water shot into his nose and forced his arms up above his head. His feet didn't touch the bottom before he began to rise again, breaking the surface with a loud gasp for air.

Matt's heart pounded and adrenaline coursed

through him. His skin stung from the impact, but the cool water washed over him like a whisper.

He felt . . . awake. Alert. Pumped.

It was the most fun thing Matt remembered doing in months—or maybe even in his entire life.

"Pretty great, right?" Dev asked, water dripping off his face.

"Pretty great," Matt said. "I want to go again."

"Well, that's easier said than done, man. You have to get back up there first." Dev pointed to the top of the cliff they had just jumped from. "And not on the path. You have to go up the hard way—that's the rule."

"The rule?" Matt swallowed the lump in his throat. It looked a lot farther going up than it had felt on the way down.

"Hi, Matt." It was a voice he'd heard back at school. Matt turned and saw one of the girls from PE. Her long brown hair was now pulled back in a ponytail, and Matt could see the freckles on her cheeks as she dog-paddled close by. "I'm Amaiya."

Matt froze, and his mind went blank. He was suddenly very aware of his wet hair plastered to the side of his face. Amaiya stared at him, waiting for a reply.

"Okay," Matt finally blurted out.

Okay?! he scolded himself. *Seriously?*

Without another word, Amaiya swam away.

A slippery volleyball whacked Matt in the side of the head. He looked around and realized he was right in the middle of a messy, net-less volleyball game. Matt spiked the ball back, planting it neatly between two players, who immediately began arguing about who had missed it.

Matt swam away from the game and watched three kids climb out of the water to dry themselves on the rocky banks. Several other kids were starting the climb back up to the top of the boulder. One by one, they propped their toes onto tiny outcroppings, sliding their fingers into narrow cracks in the rock. Slowly, carefully, they made their way upward. It was just like climbing the wall in PE, Matt thought—if the wall were a rounded, rough-sided boulder instead of a flat surface, and if he hadn't worn a harness.

"You ready to try?" Dev paddled up behind him.

"I don't know." Matt groaned. It looked pretty steep. But he *really* wanted to jump off that boulder again.

"Go for it."

Matt swam to the bank and climbed out. He shook the water off his hands.

He exhaled slowly and looked at the vertical face above him, wondering what, exactly, he had gotten himself into. A giant pit had carved itself out in his stomach. He was scared—but for some reason, he liked the feeling. It was one thing to jump off a cliff. It was another thing to climb back up it.

But that's what you did in a new place, right? You went all in.

Matt ran his hands across the uneven surface of the rock. He jammed a toe into a small dip and tested his grip just like he had in class. Perfect. He reached up with his right hand, felt around for a lip that was wide enough for his fingertips. Bingo.

He raised the other leg, then the other arm. And slowly, he began to climb. Everything and everyone else around him fell away. He was in a tunnel, alone, with only one way forward: up.

Matt inched his way toward the top. He forced himself to breathe steadily, slowly. The muscles in his forearms and thighs shook from the exertion. He had stopped to rest on a wide ledge when Amaiya went flying past him on her way down, back into the water. In the time it had taken Matt to get halfway up, she had made it to the top and leaped back in.

Next, a boy sailed by, hollering with glee. Matt paused to watch the rest of the kids jump. Dev suddenly appeared in his peripheral vision, about ten feet away, moving upward—quickly.

"Nice going, Matt!" Dev said. Matt appreciated the encouragement—but he couldn't help noticing that Dev, who had started after him, was zipping right past.

Dev was an incredible climber. He moved confidently, seemingly without pausing before each move. Yet he was a careful and smart climber too—not reckless. Matt watched as Dev reached the top and scrambled over the curved edge of the boulder.

Dev looked back down at Matt. "You got this!" he called.

"Maybe," Matt called back, "but not like you got it! That was incredible."

"Nah." Dev shrugged. "I've just climbed this route like a thousand times."

It was official: Matt was hooked on rock climbing, and he wanted to be as good a climber as Dev and the others were. If climbing the same route over and over was what he had to do to get there, then that's what he would do.

Matt hadn't meant to make any new friends in

Silver Valley, but he couldn't help it: He really liked Dev, Amaiya, and the others. And he wanted to come back here with them and climb until he got better. He'd keep climbing until he got higher, faster.

Matt tuned back in to the rock in front of him and started to think about his next move.

"Come on up, Matt," Amaiya called down from above. She had climbed back up *again*.

Matt looked up toward her voice and suddenly noticed the position of the sun in the sky. It had shifted—a lot. A bolt of panic shot through him. If he didn't hustle, he was going to be late to meet his mom.

Matt assessed the remaining distance between himself and the top of the cliff. It was a tough stretch, and this was literally his second time climbing—ever. Doing it in a hurry would just be stupid.

He looked down at the water below.

Jumping would be the fastest solution. Then he could walk the path to the top of the boulders to get his stuff.

"You stuck, dude?" Dev called down.

"No."

"'Cause you look stuck. It's cool, man. This is hard—you've done great for a first-timer."

"I'm okay," Matt said.

Dev shot him a devilish grin. "Well, then you better keep going!"

Matt shook his head and laughed. Dev was totally messing with him. Even though they'd just met, it was like Dev knew that, for better or worse, Matt had never been one to back down from a challenge.

And Dev had thrown down the challenge.

Nope, Matt thought. *I am* not *taking the easy way.*

Matt stretched out his right arm and started to close his fingers around a small wedge of rock. He gently pulled himself up, at the same time flexing his foot and pushing up on his toes, which rested on a wide but thin lip of stone.

It worked—at first. Matt was moving and he was thinking about his next hold.

Then, without warning, the pads of his fingertips slipped, and Matt's weight shifted backward. He wind-milled his arms in the air wildly as he felt himself pull away from the rock. And then he was airborne, totally detached from the rock face, and falling . . . falling . . . falling . . . with no ability to see or know when—or where—he was going to land.

"Whoa!" Dev yelled out. "Clear the decks, people!"

A chorus of squeals rose up from below. Matt heard splashing as the other kids swam out of his way.

Maybe, Matt thought, squeezing his eyes shut in anticipation of smacking into the water with a loud flop any second, *maybe I need some more practice before trying that again.*

He hit the water, and a million tiny bubbles rose up all around him.

6

IT WAS SATURDAY MORNING, AND MATT'S plan to sleep late had been foiled. His mom's voice carried from the living room—it sounded like she was on the phone. He rolled over and pulled a pillow over his head, trying to block out the noise. He peered at the clock on his nightstand. It was only six A.M.

A week had passed since Matt had tried to climb the ravine. Closing his eyes, Matt replayed his attempted ascent for about the millionth time. He pictured every crevice and crack, second-guessed every toe-hold he had rested his foot on. Once he had figured out exactly where he had gone wrong, he could try again.

Matt couldn't wait to get back there—he just hadn't had the time yet.

He rolled over onto the other side and willed himself back to sleep.

No dice.

After ten minutes of flopping around in bed like a breaching whale, Matt gave up. He threw off the covers and padded downstairs in his pajamas.

His mom was standing at the kitchen counter in full uniform, holding her cell phone tightly to her ear with one hand and rubbing her eyes with the other.

"Uh-huh," she said to the person on the other end. "Uh-huh. And how long to get there?" She looked at her watch, then listened for a second, nodding steadily. "Okay. Army Corps will be there in fifteen. Scramble the troops—I want boots on the ground by oh six thirty."

She hung up the phone and looked up to find Matt standing by the door, watching her.

"Morning, Mattie," she said with a quick smile.

"Morning, Ma. What's up?"

She let out a long, deep sigh and shook her head a little. "We've got a situation west of here. I have to leave ASAP to go inspect the old Stampede Dam, right over the border in California. With all the extra snowmelt this year, the reservoir is already filled beyond capacity. Now the dam's at risk of overflowing." Matt's mom paused and checked her phone as it pinged with a new update.

"What happens if the dam overflows?" Matt asked, rubbing sleep out of his eyes.

His mom twisted up her mouth like she was trying to figure out how—or whether—to explain something. Matt's parents always tried to tell him the truth, even if it was scary.

"If Stampede Dam overflows, then the dam wall could fail," his mom said. "And if that happens, then it would be too much water for the spillway to handle. The floodwater would flow down to Boca Dam a few miles south. And if Boca Dam fails . . . well, then all that water is going to head for Reno and Sparks . . ." She trailed off.

"Where all the people are."

She nodded. "Where all the people are."

"Wow." Matt tried to process his mom's words. "So everyone who lives there . . ." He couldn't finish the thought out loud.

"That's right, Matt. So, I need to get over there and meet the governors and the Army Corps of Engineers. We'll assess the situation—fast—and if need be, it's going to be up to the National Guard to evacuate everyone in the water's path."

Matt wasn't sure he wanted to ask the question that burned in his mind. But he had to. "We're in the path, aren't we, Mom?"

She pressed her lips tightly together. "We're east of Reno. We should be far enough away from the dams to be out of the flood path," she said. "It's the people west of us who are in immediate danger. A lot of crazy things would have to happen for the water to get this far—and for you and Bridget to be at risk."

Matt swallowed the lump that had risen in his throat.

"I don't know what's going to happen." She put a hand on his shoulder. "But I know it's going to be okay. The best and smartest and most dedicated people in the state are on this, buddy. But I could be out there for a while. Keep your phone on you at all times so I can reach you, okay?"

"Okay."

"And if the phones go out for any reason—"

"I know, I know. Don't wait for each other—just get to the safest possible place."

She kissed the top of his head, then snatched up her bag from the floor and threw it over her shoulder.

"I've got to get to the kennel. We're taking the dogs."

"Scout, too?" Matt asked, a hopeful note in his voice.

His mom turned to him. "He's . . . not quite ready yet," she said carefully.

"What does that mean?" Matt hadn't seen Scout all week, and when he'd asked his mom about the dog, she'd been vague. Now she shot him a concerned look.

"I've been wanting to tell you this," she said, "but there hasn't been a good time." She took a breath. "We're sending Scout back to Mississippi."

"What? No!" Matt practically shouted. "What are you talking about? He's a great dog—he's totally got what it takes. You just can't see it. He just needs time and some practice."

"Matt—"

"No!"

"Matt."

Matt stared at the floor and clenched and unclenched his fists. His mom seemed surprised at the intensity of his reaction.

"Matt, honey. Look at me."

Matt averted his gaze for as long as he dared, but he had never been very good at defying his parents. He looked up at his mom.

"I'm disappointed too," she said, "but Scout's just not cut out for the job. It's not good for us or for him to keep pretending. Sometimes in life we have to do what's best, which is not necessarily what we want to do. That's just how life works."

"Fine." Matt stormed across the room. "But for the record, I think you're wrong about Scout."

His mom sighed. "Duly noted," she said with a shake of her head. She shifted the weight of her pack on her shoulder. Matt could tell he had strained her patience. "My team is waiting—I have to go. Listen to Bridget while I'm gone. She's in charge."

"Okay."

"I love you, Matt."

Matt didn't respond. He stormed upstairs to his room and slammed the door.

Matt paced his room until he cooled off. He sat

down on his bed and put his head in his hands. He even surprised himself with his reaction to the news.

A hot flare of guilt went off in Matt's chest.

He'd been so distracted by rock climbing and the new friends he was making that he hadn't spent time with Scout all week—plus Scout had been in heavy training at the K-9 facility.

Matt had counted on getting to spend time with the dog over the weekend, but now they were just going to ship him back to where he came from, like a package being returned to sender?

He'd wasted the last few days he'd ever have with Scout.

Unless Matt could convince them not to send him back home.

They were wrong about Scout. He was sure of it. All he had to do was get the dog to show them what he was capable of.

And that's exactly what he was going to do.

The kennel was weirdly quiet when Matt walked in. All the other dogs—not to mention people—had been called to duty.

"Hey, Matt," the security guard at the front desk said with a wave. He was the lone staffer still at the K-9 facility. "Your mom's not here, you know."

"Yep, I know." Matt tried to remember the story he had come up with on the ride over. "She asked me to check on Scout—you know, the dog who's still here?"

"Oh yeah . . ." The guard shook his head sympathetically. "That sweet guy." He jerked his thumb in the direction of the kennels.

Matt headed past the desk and down the hallway before the guard had the chance to ask any questions.

"You know where to go?" the man called out to him.

"All good!" Matt shouted over his shoulder. "Thanks."

Matt made his way through the empty building. His footsteps rang out extra loud on the shining linoleum floor. As he moved down the hallway toward the back of the building, Matt thought he heard a sound. He froze, but the sound stopped. He took a few steps and the sound started again. He froze again, his foot hanging in midair.

It was whimpering.

He recognized it.

Matt took off at a run toward the kennels. The large

room with its bright overhead lights and rows of metal cages was uninhabited except for one dog: Scout.

Scout was frantic in his crate, whining and barking in a high-pitched tone, hopping around wildly and spinning in circles. When he caught Matt's scent, he pressed his nose through the bars and let out a series of barks that were equal parts demanding and desperate.

Matt approached the cage. "Shhhh." He didn't want the guard to hear them. As Matt fumbled with the latch, Scout's body language changed from stressed and anxious to wriggling with excitement. "Easy, pal. Easy." Matt slid the latch and swung open the door. Scout practically vaulted onto him, his front paws on Matt's shoulders. Matt stumbled backward but caught himself. He wrapped his arms around Scout in a big hug. "Okay, boy." He laughed. "I got you."

Scout was wagging his tail so hard that Matt's heart nearly broke. How could anyone not see that this dog was special?

"It's okay, Scout," Matt said, holding on tightly as the dog snuffled and nudged at his neck, then proceeded to clean Matt's face from ear to ear, chin to forehead. "It's okay. You're with me now."

7

SCOUT WAS A SLOW BUT CAREFUL MOVER. He sniffed at everything—every inch of sidewalk, every tree, every signpost. Matt tried to be patient, but he didn't want anyone to see him with the dog.

Once out of sight of the K-9 facility, Matt hopped on his bike and Scout trotted along beside him. Matt wanted to get off base and out to the desert as quickly as possible, where they'd be away from watchful eyes. Plus, for Matt to follow through on his plan, he needed open space.

He'd decided that, just like he needed to practice his rock climbing, Scout needed to train harder. If Matt could work with Scout one-on-one and get the dog to focus without distraction, he was positive he could make a difference in Scout's behavior.

He'd do everything he could to keep Scout in Nevada with him, even if it meant bending a few rules.

A couple of miles down a quiet back road that cut through the desert outside of town, Matt pulled to a stop. There were no houses or businesses—only low rocks and spiny trees as far as he could see.

"Scout, sit." Scout sat, and Matt was about to give him another command when he heard a familiar voice behind him.

"What's up, Matt!"

Matt's head swung around in surprise. He felt like he'd just been shaken awake. It took him a second to understand who he was looking at in what felt like the middle of nowhere.

"Dev? What're you doing way out here?" Matt asked, hoping Scout wouldn't call too much attention to himself.

Dev was on his bike. He had a full pack weighing down his back, with a pair of climbing shoes dangling from the straps.

"I just texted you—we're going climbing. Don't you want to come?"

"Oh, that's okay. I'm just going for a walk," Matt said.

They both looked down at the dog who waited patiently at Matt's knee. Scout turned his head from one to the other, as if he was following along with the conversation.

"That's the dog who's not yours, right?"

"Um. Right." Matt hesitated for a second.

"Isn't he a National Guard dog?"

Matt could tell this was about to go downhill fast. It was best to just admit the truth and hope Dev could be trusted. "Actually, can you keep a secret?" Matt said.

Dev shrugged. "Sure."

"Scout *does* belong to the K-9 unit. I didn't steal him, but—"

"Whoa—" Dev held out his hands to stop Matt.

"No, it's okay. He's my mom's dog—well, I mean, she works with him. And I sort of . . . uh . . . borrowed him."

"How do you borrow a dog?"

"Well, I'm going to bring him back."

"What are you planning to do with him until then?"

"Train him."

Dev crouched down on the ground and held out his hand to Scout. Scout ignored it. He looked up at Matt but didn't move.

"Uh—I think he's waiting for your command or something," Dev said.

He was right. "Okay, Scout," he said.

Scout hopped to his feet and, tail wagging, walked to Dev's outstretched hand. He sniffed Dev's fingers and wrist and made his way up Dev's arm. Dev scratched at his haunches with both hands and—in a goofy cartoon voice—said, "Who's a good boy? Who's a good boy? Scout's a good boy!"

Scout loved the attention. He wriggled and wagged, which only made Dev talk sillier and scratch more. Finally, Scout dropped to the ground, rolled over on his back, and let Dev scratch his belly.

After a few minutes, Scout rolled back onto his side and—as if nothing had happened—began nonchalantly licking his back leg.

Dev stood up. "Awesome dog. So why are you training him if he's already a National Guardsdog or whatever?"

"Well, he was going to be a K-9 search-and-rescue dog. He was flown in from Mississippi because he's supposed to be one of the best."

"And you know how to train dogs?"

Matt shook his head. "Not really—it's kind of . . . complicated."

It struck Matt how crazy this whole scene must seem to Dev. He was in the middle of the desert with a dog that didn't belong to him, trying to train him— even though Matt wasn't qualified for that task at all. He decided he needed to explain to Dev what he—and Scout—were up against.

"Here's the thing about Scout . . ." Matt began.

By the time Matt was finished with his story, Dev was looking at him in shock.

"So . . ." Dev said. "If you don't get him into shape, your mom is going to send him back to Mississippi."

"Exactly."

"Well, that's not cool. Show me what he's got, then."

Matt looked up and down the road. There were no cars in sight. He looked around at the dry, rocky desert terrain that surrounded them. This was as good a place as any.

"You want to teach Dev something?" Matt said to Scout. "Huh, buddy? C'mon, Scout!"

Scout hopped to his feet and looked up at Matt expectantly, his mouth open and his tongue lolling to the side.

"Scout, sit!" Matt spoke firmly and clearly, and he held out his hand palm up, then raised it like he was throwing something over his shoulder—the hand signal for the *sit* command.

Scout sat.

Matt turned his back to Scout and walked ten paces away. He kept his back to the dog and counted to ten. Slowly, he turned back around. Scout was watching him carefully, his head cocked to the side, his ears pricked up, and his long, fluffy tail curving out and back. But he hadn't moved.

Matt took one big step to his left.

Scout followed him with his eyes.

Matt took one giant step backward.

Scout watched him from his spot.

"Okay, Scout!" Matt said. Scout leaped to his feet and ran over to Matt in one smooth motion. He was at Matt's feet within a second. He sat back down, his eyes locked on Matt, and waited for his next command.

"That's amazing!" Dev exclaimed. "My dog? You tell him to lie down and he stands up."

"Watch this!" Matt was getting into working with Scout now. "Scout, sit," Matt said. Matt scanned the area around them and spotted an oddly bent tree about ten yards ahead and off to the right. Lowering his voice and making it sound serious, like Sergeant Klein the K-9 handler had taught him, he looked in the direction of the tree, raised his hand to point at it, and said, "Go out!"

Scout stood up, turned in the direction Matt was pointing, took a step forward, and hesitated. He looked back at Matt, as if he needed reassurance. Matt kept his gaze locked on the spot and his hand extended. He waited a beat, giving Scout time to respond. When Scout didn't move, he gave the command once more.

Something clicked in Scout. The dog turned to face forward and made a beeline in the direction Matt was looking and pointing. All signs of uncertainty were gone. Scout stepped confidently, sniffing at the air and lowering his nose to the ground as he walked.

"What's he going to do?" Dev whispered.

"You don't have to whisper." Matt laughed. "And hopefully he's going to stop when I tell him to. But we'll see."

Matt watched Scout closely. Would he listen when they were out here in the open, instead of inside the training facility?

When the dog was a foot from the tree, Matt sucked in his breath and firmly commanded: "Stop!"

Not only did Scout *not* stop, but he totally lost all focus. His whole body relaxed, and he slowed to a crawl. His nose skimming the ground, he meandered toward the tree, then around it, then off at an angle away from the sidewalk.

Matt and Dev burst out laughing.

"Still, not bad," Dev said.

"Like I said—he needs some work." Matt whistled at Scout. Scout's ears swung around toward the sound, but he continued sniffing at the ground and taking a leisurely tour of the area.

Dev's phone jingled in his pocket.

"Yeah—sorry," he said as he picked it up, "I got distracted. On my way." He clicked off the call. "Do you want to come check out Howler's Peak?" Dev asked.

"Howler's Peak?"

"It's a climbing spot, better than the ravine. The routes aren't even vertical—they're practically horizontal." Dev held his hand out parallel to the ground. His eyes lit up with excitement. "It's beyond cool. I have some extra shoes and gear you could use. But . . ." Dev paused. "I don't want to take you away from Scout or anything."

Matt didn't know what to do. He was desperate to

get Scout in top shape before his mom came back from the dam. But he had also been waiting to go climbing for a week. And Howler's Peak sounded amazing.

As Dev talked, Matt felt a familiar sensation growing in his chest. He tried to will it away—it was a feeling that had gotten him in trouble many times before: impatience. Matt didn't want to wait until he had climbed a million easy routes before trying a harder, cooler route. He didn't want to miss out on a day with his friends, doing the thing he had started to love.

This was the impatience that pushed Matt to do things he wasn't quite capable of doing yet. That, in Texas, made him try to jump a wide stream on his bike. That, in Maine, motivated him to sled down a hill so steep it should have been called a wall.

He wanted to be just as good as Dev at climbing, but he wanted it *now*.

"It's serious business," Dev went on. "There are a couple of easier routes, but mostly it's, like, *really* hard. I don't know . . ."

Matt grinned. He couldn't help himself. "Let's go."

8

HALF AN HOUR LATER, MATT AND DEV pulled up on their bikes, huffing and puffing, at a flat, wide-open spot in the desert that was sprinkled with rock formations in every shape, width, and height. Scout was only panting slightly after the long run alongside Matt's bike. In fact, he seemed to have enjoyed the exercise.

"*That's* Howler's," Dev said grandly, his voice full of awe. He pointed at a short stack of boulders set down in a small basin. The stack was squat and wide and the middle section bulged out sideways—like peanut butter squishing out from inside a sandwich.

With a name like Howler's Peak, Matt had expected

a towering skyscraper of rock that blocked out the sun. He couldn't help but laugh.

"It doesn't look like much, right?" Dev shook his head. "But trust me—those routes are incredibly hard. You see that overhang?"

Matt saw it. Scattered across the face of Howler's were Amaiya, Curtis, and a few other kids. Amaiya clung to the side of the rock, practically upside down, and her ponytail hung straight toward the ground. The climbers lay nearly flat, with their backs to the ground and their faces turned up to the sky. They hung on to the rock face like Spider-Man clones, defying the laws of gravity.

More kids were on the ground, manning the ropes attached to the climbers and calling up encouragement. Big foam pads were strewn across the ground to protect the climbers if they fell.

Even more amazing than the sight of Howler's Peak was the sight of all these kids climbing it—seemingly with ease. As Dev buckled himself into his harness and slipped on his climbing shoes, Matt studied the climbers. He observed their techniques, their movements, the choices they made on the face of the rock.

The first thing Matt noticed was that the climbers were taking their time—they weren't in a rush. It was also pretty clear that they had been working on these routes for a long time.

He watched as Amaiya studied a tiny crack in the rock above her head for a moment before gently gripping it with just the pads of her fingers. She tried it out but wasn't satisfied with it. So instead of trying to find another way straight up, she did what smart climbers do—she checked out her options to the left and right.

Sometimes the best way up wasn't *up* at all.

After feeling around for a bit, Amaiya settled on a hold to her left instead. She moved sideways and clipped into a carabiner attached to a bolt that was screwed into the rock. Then she checked her line and exchanged a few words with the boy spotting her from below. She repeated these steps slowly, moving along at a steady but controlled pace.

Dev handed Matt a pair of climbing shoes. "These your size?"

Matt's throat had gone dry. He was equal parts nervous and excited—and entirely determined to start climbing as soon as possible. He took the shoes from Dev's hand. "Looks like it."

"I'd start with that route," Dev said, pointing to a stubby mass of rock to their right. "That's where we all started."

It was a short, rotund boulder sitting on the ground, with another boulder lodged squarely on top. They looked like two oversize scoops of ice cream. The stack was only about eight feet high, and it had a bumpy face with several outcroppings that would make perfect holds.

In other words, it was an easy climb.

Matt didn't want an easy climb.

"That's cool," Matt said. "But I think I'll start over there." He pointed toward Amaiya and the other kids.

Dev shot Matt a look that said *You're crazy.* "Are you sure that's a good idea?"

"Gotta start somewhere, right?"

"Yeah—over there." Dev pointed toward the ice-cream scoops. He shook his head. "*That's* where you start, man."

"Don't worry," Matt said. "I'll be fine."

"Well, at least let me get you the right equipment, then." Dev turned toward the kids gathered at the base of the rock. "Anyone have an extra harness and helmet?"

"Here you go." A boy Matt recognized from social

studies tossed the gear at them.

Matt caught it. He stepped through the large loop that went around his waist and above his hips, and stuck each foot through one of the leg loops. Dev helped him check the buckles and pull the straps tighter. Matt clipped the helmet snugly under his chin.

He bent down to put the flexible, rubber-soled climbing shoes on, but they felt at least two sizes too small. His toes curled up under themselves. "Youch!"

"They're supposed to be like that," Dev said. "That means they fit."

"If you say so." Matt hobbled awkwardly toward the rock. Scout followed closely behind him, sniffing at the shoes and the strange webbing wrapped around Matt's body.

Dev grabbed one end of a long rope. He made a few knots in it, then a loop. He fed the loop into a small metal device. Dev clipped it to the carabiner dangling from the front of Matt's harness.

"Once you start making moves, clip your rope into the carabiners attached to the rock. The other end of that rope will be attached to me, and I'll keep letting out slack for you," Dev said. "And if you fall, I'll catch you. Got it?"

"Wait—what do you do if you're alone?" Matt asked. "How do you climb without someone on the ground?"

"If you're alone"—Dev held up a different metal device that hung from Matt's belt—"you use this one instead. It has a brake on it. But please promise me you won't be needing that anytime soon?"

"I promise."

Dev eyed him skeptically.

"Let's do this!" Matt swallowed hard and wiped his hands on his shorts.

A small bag dangled from the harness on Matt's right side. Matt touched it, and a puff of white powder escaped and floated away on the breeze.

"What's this?"

"Chalk. Use it to keep your hands dry."

Matt nodded.

Scout nudged at Matt's knee.

"It's okay, bud," Matt said, scratching the top of Scout's head. "It's just climbing gear. I'm going to go up there"—he pointed to the top of the boulder—"and then I'll come back down for you. Okay?"

Scout answered by exhaling sharply through his nose and studying Matt's face carefully, as if he were searching for a reason why Matt would do something so stupid. Matt smiled at the dog. "I swear. I'll be right back. Sit."

Scout sat.

Matt took a deep breath, exhaled, and began his first ascent of Howler's Peak. It was slow going at first, but he focused closely on the surface of the rock in front of him. He wasn't fully horizontal, but he was angled backward, hanging down from the rock like he was floating in midair.

Just like he had at the ravine, Matt tried to think of the bumps and ridges in the stone face as plastic holds in the climbing wall at school. This wasn't any harder, he told himself. Just different.

Matt kept his eyes from what was above or below him and only thought about the next hold. Little by little, he made his way along the route.

"Nice, Matt!" Dev shouted from below. "Slow and steady!"

The other kids had reached the top and pulled themselves up onto a ledge above. He could barely see around the overhang of the boulder he was climbing, but they could see him. They looked down and shouted encouragement.

"You got this!"

"Keep going, Matt!"

Scout chimed in with one loud bark from below.

Matt was about halfway up when he sensed more than saw something off to his left. He waited until he was secure in his position, then turned his head to look over. It was Curtis, and he was scrambling up the side of the boulder—fast. He had started a few minutes after Matt but was already parallel to him. Matt couldn't believe the speed at which Curtis was moving. His legs and arms stretched out in all directions.

Matt watched Curtis until he disappeared from view around the top of the rounded boulder. Matt heard the sound of high fives above him.

Matt's attention returned to his own position on the rock. He was starting to get tired. He closed his eyes and took a couple of deep breaths. When he opened them, he saw that the entire group of kids above had moved around to the side, where they had a better view of his climb.

A strange sensation passed through Matt's body—a hot-cold combination of awkwardness, embarrassment, discomfort . . . and uncertainty.

What was he thinking? There was no way he could make this climb.

Suddenly, Matt felt completely unsure of himself.

His arms started shaking with fatigue. He became aware of the muscles in his calves starting to twitch and complain a little.

"You good?" Dev called up.

"All good," Matt replied, hoping he sounded more confident than he felt.

"Dude, you don't have to do this, you know," Dev said. "It's really hard—none of us got it on our first try either."

Dev wasn't egging Matt on this time. He really meant it.

"I got this," Matt said. One at a time, he stuffed his hands into the chalk bag and rubbed them in the powder.

Matt reached out for his next hold. He slid his fingertips into a dip in the rock and pulled down a little, testing the position. It felt sturdy. He looked over and positioned his hand, then looked down and found a hold for each foot. He was ready to move. He exhaled deeply and shifted his weight to his right foot, then pulled with his right fingertips.

Without warning, Matt's fingers slipped off the rock and his arm flew out to his side. Adrenaline shot through him as his reflexes kicked in. He reached up and grabbed at the rock, his fingers grappling for a hold—any hold—that would keep him from falling. He got lucky. He managed to latch on to a small bump that was barely big enough to hold him.

Matt had caught himself just in time.

Down below, Scout began to bark—once, twice, then repeatedly. It was a worried sound, a protective call to action. But there was nothing Scout could do to help Matt. Matt had to figure this one out on his own.

Matt's heart was pounding hard. He wasn't sure if it was from the near fall, the weight of all those eyes on him, or both. He had a rope to catch him, so it wasn't like he was going to fall the ten feet to the ground. But still.

He took a few breaths to steady himself.

"Try to your left," Amaiya called out from above. "A little higher."

The sound of her voice sent a current of anxiety through Matt's gut. He tried to ignore it and looked toward the spot she had suggested. He strained to see above his hand. There was a deep crevice he hadn't seen before. He stretched his arm as far as it could go and just managed to slip his fingertips in and grab on. Now he had to find a place for the rest of his limbs. His arms were really starting to shake. Matt hated to admit it, but he wasn't going to be able to hold on much longer.

A bead of sweat dripped down Matt's face and fell onto the ground below with a solid splat.

He needed to go faster.

"Matt—go to your left again," Dev directed him. But Matt had spied a nice wide hold to his right. He ignored Dev and reached for it. "Seriously, Matt, that's not a good route—there's nowhere to go on the right. Trust me, please. You're just going to have to come back down and do what I'm telling you to do now, or you'll tire yourself out."

Matt didn't doubt that the left hold would work. But he didn't see any reason that the right one couldn't work too. Maybe no one else had done it properly yet. There was only one way to find out.

He straightened his legs, pushing himself up from his knees, and pulled with his fingers. It was working: He was moving upward and slightly to the side, finally making progress again.

Relief washed over him. His confidence started to

come back. Matt moved his feet up to new, higher spots on the rock and began to reach upward again with his left hand. As he did, he felt the small bit of rock under his right foot start to give. With a short, sharp *pop!* the rock snapped off and clattered to the ground beneath him.

Matt couldn't hold on. His other foot slipped off its perch and his right arm slid from its hold. His left hand started to come off the rock too, but his forefinger was wedged too far into the crevice. As he fell, his finger twisted and bent sideways. Matt let out a cry of pain. Just when he thought his finger was going to break, he managed to yank it free.

Now he was falling.

Matt plunged downward, bouncing off the face of Howler's Peak as he fell.

It didn't matter that he was wearing a harness. It didn't matter that the harness was connected to a rope, or that the rope was firmly attached to Dev, or even that Matt had hooked himself to the rock. In that instant, Matt felt as if nothing would stop him from crashing into the hard ground below. He could feel it as though it were already happening.

He was just grateful for the foam pads that would

hopefully soften the blow.

At the last second, the rope held.

Dev used all his weight to keep Matt aloft. Matt jerked to a stop a few feet from the ground, but not before whacking his knee into the stone face. He let out another yelp of pain.

Scout barked frantically from below, and all the kids cried out from above.

"Are you okay?"

"Dude!"

"Matt—you good?"

Matt's whole body was shaking from shock. He took a couple of breaths, then an inventory of which body parts were already starting to ache, throb, and burn. His finger hurt—a lot—but he could move it. His knee was red and scraped and bleeding, but bendable. Every part of him seemed to be in working order—except his self-esteem.

Matt would have given anything at that moment for a cave to suddenly open up in the rock in front of him, so he could crawl inside and stay there until everyone else went away.

But that wasn't going to happen. Instead, he raised a hand over his head and gave a thumbs-up. Cheers from above echoed all around him.

Matt heard a scratching and scuttling sound beneath him. He twisted his body to look and saw Scout trying to scramble up the side of the rock to reach him. Matt had to laugh. When Scout couldn't get to Matt that way, he ran right underneath Matt and stood up on his hind legs. Stretching his neck up, up, up, Scout was just able to touch his nose to Matt's back.

A chorus of *aaawwwwww*s rose up from the group above.

"Thanks, pal," Matt said.

"Bringing you down, okay?" Dev said. Matt nodded.

"Scout, move!" Matt said. Scout stepped aside and sat down, waiting impatiently.

Dev slowly lowered Matt to the ground, and Matt quickly undid his harness and stepped out of it. Scout ran over and sniffed at the scrape on his knee and his banged-up knuckles. Scout whimpered and sniffed, ran a half circle around Matt, then ran back in the other direction, whimpering some more.

"It's okay, Scout," Matt said. "Told you I'd be right back."

Dev put his hand on Matt's shoulder. "You sure you're all right?"

"I'm fine," Matt said. He took a step toward his backpack, and it was instantly clear that he wasn't fine at all. His knee almost gave out on him, and he winced. He clamped his mouth shut to prevent a gasp of pain from escaping.

Dev eyed him suspiciously, but let it drop.

Matt sat down right where he was. Scout immediately climbed onto his lap and started licking his face, hovering over him. Dev and the other kids on the ground gathered around and stared down at him with worried expressions on their faces. All the kids above—including Amaiya—were silent, holding their breath, hoping he was really okay.

Pinned to the ground under Scout, Matt leaned back on his hands and looked up at all the wide eyes and furrowed brows, at the concern on Dev's face.

They watched him and waited.

And he started to laugh.

Matt chuckled a little at first, but then he started to crack up. For a second the others weren't sure what was happening or what to do, but soon they started to laugh too.

"What's so funny?" Dev asked, breaking into a grin himself.

"That was such a bad idea," Matt managed to get out between cackles. "You were right," he breathed. "I never should have tried that!"

Dev started laughing too, and soon he was doubled over. "I told you so!" he choked out. "You're a really good climber, dude"—he snorted—"but a terrible listener."

"Thank you," Matt said, wiping tears from his eyes, "for stopping me from busting open my head."

"You're welcome," Dev said, shaking his head. "But, please, can you just start over there next time?" He pointed toward the easy routes.

"Promise." Matt caught his breath. His cheeks and sides hurt from laughing so hard. Somewhere under all the humor, though, he was genuinely sorry. Dev would have felt terrible if Matt had gotten more seriously hurt, and it would have been all Matt's fault. "Seriously, though, Dev"—Matt tried to stand up—"I'm sorry for being an idiot."

"It's cool." Dev stuck out a hand and carefully pulled Matt to his feet. "Maybe you should start wearing a helmet all the time though—just in case?"

"Maybe."

"Tell me something," Dev said as they headed for

their bikes, Matt limping and Dev walking slowly, still letting out peals of laughter every now and then.

"What?"

"Did you do crazy stuff like this in every place you've lived?"

Matt thought about that for a second. "Sort of."

"Huh." Dev shrugged. "So it's just you, not Nevada?"

Scout stayed close as Matt hobbled along, his head brushing against Matt's hand as they walked. Matt was grateful for Scout's loyalty. The dog didn't care that he was acting like a total moron, or that he had just made a fool out of himself. All he cared about was that Matt was okay.

Wasn't that what true friends were for?

9

THE PAIN SEEPED INTO HIS DREAMS. Matt emerged from a deep sleep the next morning into a state of serious achiness.

He opened his eyes. It was Sunday, and the sun was shining brightly through the blinds on his windows. Matt sat up. His finger was throbbing, his knee was stiff and sore, and a thousand tiny scrapes burned up and down the front of his body. But overall, nothing hurt as badly as he had feared.

Matt swung his legs to the side and put his feet on the floor. He kicked something warm and furry—Scout. The dog had slept by his side all night long. Matt reached down and gave Scout a scratch behind the ears. Scout leaped to his feet and dropped his head onto Matt's lap.

"Good morning," Matt said. Scout raised his eyes to look up at him.

Matt checked his phone for any more news from his mom. He hadn't heard from her since the night before, after he got home from Howler's. She'd texted to say that the dams were holding—for now. They still weren't out of the woods, though, and she wanted to stay on-site.

She hadn't sent any updates since then.

Standing up was a chore, but Matt took a few steps and shook out his stiff limbs. He stepped over the borrowed climbing harness, helmet, and shoes, which he had accidentally brought home with him. They lay on the floor where he'd thrown them down the afternoon before. In the confusion after he hurt himself, he'd forgotten to return them.

He hobbled to the door, Scout following closely behind. Just as Matt put his hand on the doorknob, though, he froze.

He couldn't take Scout downstairs—the dog was a stowaway. He'd managed to avoid Bridget yesterday, but he was sure he wouldn't be so lucky today. In fact,

Matt was amazed no one had caught onto his scheme yet.

"Sorry, pal," Matt said, opening the door just enough to squeeze through. Scout started to nose his way out of the room, but Matt blocked him with his knee—the sore one. "Stay, Scout. I'll bring you some food, okay? Just stay here and be quiet."

Scout replied with a yowling half whine, half yawn and looked up at Matt with big, sad eyes.

"That's not going to work this time." Matt leaned down and let Scout lick his face. He scratched the soft fur under Scout's chin. "Stay."

Matt shut the door softly behind him and crept—limping and wobbling—down the stairs.

Bridget sat at the kitchen table with a bowl of oatmeal and her dinging cell phone in front of her.

"Morning," she said without looking up. She laughed at something on her phone and quickly typed a reply. Matt was glad, for once, that she was ignoring him.

"Morning," he mumbled. He grabbed a bowl, cereal, and milk. While he was at the counter, he pocketed a couple of slices of bread. He gingerly sat down, and they ate in silence.

Matt chewed quickly, hoping he could get out of there before his sister looked up. He needed to get back upstairs before Scout made any noise.

Matt couldn't stop replaying what had happened at Howler's the day before. He saw the scene playing out in his head: the rock breaking under his foot, the moment he started to fall, his finger jammed in the crevice . . . He bent and straightened his finger, trying to loosen it up. Every time he saw himself dangling from the rock, he wanted to go back and try it again—and do it right this time.

But at this moment, his primary goal was making it out of the kitchen without Bridget looking up. She would take one look at him and his injuries, and she'd drag all the details out of him, like she always did. And then she'd have to tell their mom, and he'd be in serious trouble.

Without looking at him, Bridget stood up and, still staring into her phone, turned and headed for the living room. Matt held his breath. At the last second, she spun back around to look at him, about to say something.

Matt froze mid-chew, as if by sitting perfectly still maybe he would become invisible.

No luck.

Bridget's jaw fell open wide, and her eyes rounded into saucers. No sound escaped her mouth. Matt watched as her expression shifted from surprise to confusion to concern to his least favorite, anger, as she took in the extent of his injuries.

She looked like she was going to pop.

Matt couldn't take it for another second. "I'm fine," he said. "Thanks for asking."

Bridget found her voice. "What happened to you? Did someone do this to you? Who hurt you? You can tell me, Matt—"

"Bridge," he cut her off. "No one did this to me. Breathe."

"Then what the heck happened? Did you get in a fight with the sidewalk or something?"

Matt knew his sister was not going to let him get out of the conversation without a good explanation—and Scout was waiting for him upstairs. He decided the quickest solution was to tell her the truth.

"I climbed Howler's Peak. Well, I tried to climb it."

Her face twisted up into something between parental and curious. "Do I even want to know what Howler's Peak is?" Before Matt could come up with a reply, she tapped at her phone and pulled up pictures of it. Her mouth fell open again, and she turned the phone around so he could see the photos she was seeing.

"Matt! What the— What were you thinking? This is, like, for serious climbers! You've never gone rock climbing before in your life!"

"Well, I almost got to the top of the climbing wall in PE?" he offered sheepishly. "And I climbed most of a boulder at the ravine the other day?"

"The rav— What?" Bridget's stinging glare shut him up. Matt heard a scuffling sound overhead. Scout was getting restless. Luckily, Bridget's blood seemed to be boiling so loud in her ears that she didn't notice. She stepped closer to Matt and exhaled. She squeezed her eyes shut, and when she opened them again, her face had softened.

"Matt, are you okay? For real?"

"I'm fine. Just sore, but it's nothing serious."

She shook her head and rolled her eyes. "What happened?"

Matt exhaled slowly. And then the whole story just came pouring out of him.

Matt told his sister all about Dev and his group of

friends. He told her about how they had gone to the ravine together, and how Dev and the others had said Matt was a really good climber.

He told Bridget how he had not only failed to get to the top of Howler's, but he had fallen. He detailed his injuries—and how he'd dangled there, shocked and in pain, while all the other kids watched. And then he told her that he'd surprised himself and everyone else by having an uncontrollable laughing fit. So now they thought he was a reckless person, a bad climber, *and* a weirdo.

When he was done talking, Matt felt better. And also worse. Telling Bridget what happened was like putting down something heavy that he'd been carrying for a long time. But saying the words out loud was also a solid reminder of his poor choices—and that he'd let his impatience get the best of him.

Bridget whistled softly. "That sucks."

"Yeah," was all Matt could say.

"Okay, let's forget for a second that Mom is going to kill me for letting this happen to you. You really have to be more careful, Matt. People are still going to like you even if you don't do, like, the hardest and most dangerous thing possible. You know that, right?"

Matt just shrugged. He looked at the floor, then at the wall, then at the floor again—anywhere but at Bridget.

Bridget was watching him, a pained look on her face. "Matt, what's going on? Everywhere we've ever lived you've just settled right in. But this time it seems harder. What's the deal?"

She was right. This move was harder, but Matt wasn't sure why. Maybe it was because his mom was working all the time now. Maybe it was because this was his dad's third deployment in a few years. Or maybe it was because Bridget was a straight-A student with a gajillion friends—not to mention that she was seventeen and starting to think about college.

They had always been in it together, as a family. But now, for the first time in his life, Matt felt alone.

And in order to stop feeling alone, he had to go all in and start over . . . again. He had to make new friends in a new place, where he was the new kid and no one knew if he was cool or boring, funny or clueless, athletic or unskilled, smart or a terrible student.

Kids who grew up in one place spent their days with people who knew them. They didn't have to explain who they were—they just got to be themselves. But kids like Matt had to show people who they were, again and again.

They had to keep proving themselves. But every time Matt proved himself, his family moved again.

Matt really wanted this time to be the last, at least for a while. He wanted Dev, Amaiya, and the others to be the people who knew him best.

And he didn't want to do anything to mess that up.

It was like Bridget could read his mind. "It sucks to start over. Believe me, I get it. But that's not an excuse to do something really stupid. Okay?"

"Okay."

"Besides, I'm sure it wasn't nearly as bad as it felt."

Matt saw himself being lowered to the ground by Dev. "Um, I don't know about that."

"Well, even if it was horrible, it happened, right?"

Matt wasn't sure what she meant. "I guess so?"

"Meaning," Bridget went on, "it happened. It's done. You can't unscramble eggs, like Dad always says."

Matt sucked air through his teeth and shook his head. "Well—"

"Dev said himself that none of them made it to the top on the first try, right?"

"Right. But—"

"Trust me, Matt, no one freakin' cared."

Her phone buzzed and she looked at it.

"Shoot, it's late. I have to go to a study group. Can you stay out of trouble for, like, three hours?"

"I'm good."

Bridget eyed him, unconvinced. "Famous last words." She snatched up her books and her purse and headed for the front door. "Oh, one more thing. You're not going back to Howler's Peak, right?"

"Bye, Bridge. Thanks for listening."

"Matt!"

"Ever?"

"Matt."

Matt just stared at her. He didn't want to make a promise he couldn't keep.

She let out a frustrated sigh and studied him for a long moment. "You're doing fine, Matt. What's the rush? Just give yourself time, okay?"

"Thanks, Sis."

With a wave, she headed out.

A second after the front door shut behind her, Matt heard a sharp bark from upstairs.

Scout! Matt had forgotten that the dog was waiting for his breakfast. He still had the bread in his pocket—did dogs even eat bread? He grabbed a bowl from the cupboard and took the stairs two at a time.

Scout scarfed the bread down, snorting and barely chewing as he swallowed it almost whole. Matt filled the bowl with water in the bathroom, then put it down on his bedroom floor. Scout slurped it up messily.

Matt watched the dog and thought about what his sister had said. Maybe she was right—Matt didn't need to do something risky just to get people to like him. And he had to learn to be patient.

But still. He knew he could do it. He could climb Howler's. He *had* to climb Howler's.

10

AS SCOUT SNIFFED THE FLOOR IN search of even the tiniest dropped crumbs, Matt snatched up the climbing gear and shoved it into his backpack. In the kitchen, he filled a water bottle and grabbed a few protein bars. Scout sniffed at the air as Matt threw in some dog treats that he'd found in one of his mom's jacket pockets.

"I don't care what my sister says," Matt said to Scout. "We're going back to Howler's. And I'm going to nail it this time—by myself."

Scout looked up at Matt and wagged his tail. He was ready to go too.

Ignoring the scrapes and bruises that smarted all over his body, Matt hopped on his bike. They got about a mile from the base before Matt realized that he didn't know exactly where Howler's Peak was. He pulled over under a tree on a quiet residential street. It was still early in the day, but it was already getting hot. Matt wiped his brow on his sleeve. Scout sat panting nearby, his tongue dangling from his open mouth. Matt gave him some water.

Matt opened a map app on his phone and typed in his destination. It was a few miles farther. As he plotted the quickest route, a text came in from his mom.

Still here. Everything okay there? Love you, M. Be good.

Yup, all good here, Matt texted back with a pang of guilt. *I'm sorry for being mad about Scout earlier. Love you too.*

It's ok buddy. I understand. Check in with you later.

He figured out the fastest route and started off in that direction. He rode about ten yards before he realized that Scout wasn't running at his side. Matt screeched to a halt and looked back over his shoulder.

Scout was sitting right where Matt had left him, staring off into the distance. Was he looking at the clouds in the sky? At the hills outside of town?

"Scout, come."

Scout ignored him.

"Scout, *come*." Matt was firm. Still no response from the dog.

Matt knew that he'd been so focused on getting better at climbing that he'd forgotten about his promise to Scout. He'd meant to keep training him so that he wouldn't be sent back to Mississippi. Well, maybe now was his chance—maybe Scout could lead him to Howler's Peak.

Matt steered his bike back toward the dog and pulled up alongside him. Scout's ears twitched, and he opened his mouth, then snapped it shut.

It was as if Scout was tuned in to a far-off frequency that no one else could hear.

Matt tapped the dog on the top of his head. Scout flinched, then spun around and barked at Matt. It wasn't aggressive, but he was definitely trying to tell Matt something.

The problem was, Matt had no idea what that something was.

"Whoa, buddy." Matt looked around again. He was confused. What had changed in the past few minutes to make Scout behave so oddly all of a sudden?

Matt scanned the sky, the horizon line, the rocky landscape and dried shrubs that surrounded them on all sides. He pulled out his phone again and looked at the map.

Scout was looking in the direction of the Stampede and Boca Dams, where Matt's mom was working.

He looked down at Scout. The dog's gaze was locked.

Matt had a strange feeling, but he pushed it away.

"Come on, Scout." Matt pulled the climbing harness out of his backpack and held it out for Scout to sniff. The dog ran his nose up and down the nylon webbing. "Find Howler's!" Matt commanded him. Scout focused his attention back on Matt and barked as if he understood. He started to walk beside Matt's bike, leading the way. "Good boy."

Matt began to pedal and Scout ran ahead of him. Matt watched the dog's purposeful stride and then, without warning, Scout veered off to the right and bolted at top speed into the brush. A pit formed in Matt's stomach. If he lost Scout, he'd be in huge trouble. He realized that it'd been dumb not to put Scout on a leash.

"Scout! Stop!" Matt yelled, but Scout kept going. Matt swerved and took off after the dog. Spiky brush scratched at his legs as he rode. Scout was moving fast, but Matt caught up to him. "Hey!" Matt scolded him. "Scout! Stay!"

Scout finally seemed to hear him. The dog slowed to a trot, looked over his shoulder at Matt, and stopped. Matt fumbled around in his backpack for a carabiner and some rope. He clipped the carabiner around Scout's collar and knotted the rope like Dev had taught him. Then he held the rope in one hand while he got back on his bike. It wasn't a perfect leash, but it would do. Scout whimpered a little but turned to follow Matt back toward the road. Scout looked back in the direction he'd been running a couple of times, but otherwise seemed back to his usual self.

Matt was happy to see that Howler's was deserted. There was no one there to talk him out of trying to climb it again.

Using the metal belay for solo climbers that Dev had showed him, Matt clicked into his harness and connected himself to the rope attached to the rock.

He tested the brake, which would stop a fall—not that Matt planned to fall again.

Scout sat patiently by his side as Matt looked up at the short, bulging rock.

Matt's heart rate picked up speed just looking at the route he was about to climb. He replayed the moves he had tried in his first attempt, making note of what would work again—and what definitely wouldn't. He heard Dev's and the other kids' voices in his head, calling out directions and leading him to different holds.

But there was no way to know if a spot would work until you tried it. And there was no way to get to the top of a boulder without starting to climb. He dragged over a foam mat someone had left behind and angled it under his route. If he did fall, this would add some padding.

Matt looked down at Scout, who studied him mutely. The fur on top of Scout's head was furrowed, and his ears were back. His tail hung down. Scout tilted his head to the side, opened his mouth, and snapped it shut with a yowl. He looked from Matt to the rock, and back to Matt again.

"Unless you have skills like no other dog on earth," Matt said, "you can't go up there with me."

In response, Scout dropped his chest to the ground and raised his backside in the air, bowing to Matt—a pose that was an invitation to play.

"You're not going to take off on me again, are you?"

Scout responded by hopping up and running in a figure eight around Matt. Every time Scout circled past him, he brushed against Matt's legs.

"Scout!" Matt laughed, swatting the dog away. "What're you doing? Sit."

Scout stopped running. He stared at Matt. Matt stared back, waiting. Reluctantly, Scout sat.

"Good boy. Now stay."

Scout followed the command, but he strained against it. He stretched out his neck and yipped at Matt. He lifted a paw and swiped at the ground. He wiggled his bottom and started to lift it from the dirt, then sat back down.

Scout was trying to tell him something, Matt realized. But what?

He didn't have time to stick around and figure it out. He needed to climb.

Ignoring Scout's whimpers, Matt planted his hands on the face of the rock that had already been warmed by the late-morning sun. He ran his hands over its surface, letting his fingertips read the bumps and indents. He plotted his route in his head.

One of his dad's sayings came to Matt's mind just then: *Know where you're going before you start,* his dad would say, *but remember that it will change along the way. Don't be afraid to reroute.*

Matt's injured finger was killing him, and his body ached in a dozen different places. But he ignored the pain and perched the fingertips of his right hand on a small shelf of rock that jutted out about a half inch. He gently tucked the toes of his right foot into a crevice, bent his knee, and pushed up. Balancing his weight between his hand and foot, he quickly reached for a crack in the rock with his left hand and grabbed hold.

He repeated these steps—slowly, carefully, but with purpose. Every few feet, he clipped into a carabiner bolted to the rock and tested the brake. The world around him quickly fell away. Matt forgot about the conversation with his sister. He forgot that his mother had been out on a risky job for more than a day and that the last thing he'd said to her was an angry accusation. He forgot that his dad was thousands of miles away and in who knew what kind of conditions. He forgot that he was the new kid who'd had to start over yet again.

Matt knew only what his body was doing at that moment, and what it needed to do next. Slowly but surely, he made his way along the rock.

With every transfer of weight from a hand to a foot, from one hand to the other, Matt repeated a few words to himself: *I can do this, and I will do this.*

11

MATT WIPED THE SWEAT FROM HIS BROW. He looked up and, for a second, couldn't figure out where he was on the rock. He saw only reddish-gold stone inches from his face and spreading out around him in all directions.

Matt pulled his head back and refocused his eyes, trying to place himself on the curving face of Howler's. He'd been focusing so closely on every move, every finger and toe, that he hadn't added it all up.

When he did, he let out a whoop of joy.

He was almost at the top.

He wanted to charge ahead and get there as fast as he could, but his muscles were starting to shake. He stopped for a break.

Matt took a moment to look around. In the distance, tiny cars glinted on a highway that looked like a doodled line on a map. The air wavered in squiggly lines as the day heated up.

He turned his face up, toward the intense blue of the vast sky above him. He felt a soft breeze on his skin, which took the edge off the heat. He smelled the desert brush and dry earth that spread out around Howler's almost as far as he could see.

Matt allowed himself to appreciate every bit of this feeling—the same feeling he'd had when he was kayaking on the Truckee. This was his favorite place to be: outdoors, alone with just the quiet of nature.

Except there was one thing that was not quiet: the constant stream of barking coming from Scout. The barking was so steady that it had become one continuous sound, echoing off the rock and bouncing back at Matt from what felt like every side.

Scout was really not happy that Matt was climbing Howler's.

"Scout!" Matt called down. "Shush!"

Scout abruptly stopped barking. The quiet was a relief. But after a beat, Scout started up again.

Matt groaned. He just needed to finish this ascent,

then get back down to Scout. That was the only way the dog would stop the racket.

But first, he wanted to enjoy the breeze and the sunshine and the view for just a few seconds more. He turned his face to the sun and closed his eyes, listening to the gentle whoosh of the wind in his ears. It was the sound you only hear when you're high above the ground.

All of a sudden, Scout went quiet. The absence of sound was so startling that for a second, Matt's ears rang. Then, as quickly as he'd stopped barking, Scout started whimpering and howling. There was a new, desperate note to his cries.

Scout was directly below him, which made him hard to see. Matt twisted around as much as he dared and tilted his head to catch a glimpse of the dog. Scout stood up, his muscles tensed, his ears raised and rotated forward on his head. His tail stuck straight up in the air. The dog was on high alert. He was staring off into the distance, listening and watching carefully.

And that's when Matt heard a sickening sound that would haunt him forever: a piercing crack that echoed off the sky itself, like amplified lightning.

What on earth could have made that sound?

For the first time since he'd begun his climb that day, Matt was scared. He scanned the horizon as Scout howled.

Another sound—like tumbling rocks, or a mudslide—came to him on the breeze. He turned his head toward it. A terrifying thought occurred to him. Matt closed his eyes and pictured the map on his phone, locating Howler's on it like dropping a pin. He oriented himself and knew, with a terrible sinking feeling, that he was facing the same direction in which Scout had been barking earlier.

He was facing the Truckee River and the two dams. And that's where the sounds were coming from.

Just like his mom had feared, Stampede Dam was failing.

It must have overflowed, and the dam wall wasn't strong enough to hold back all the water.

Would the whole dam crumble? If it did, would Boca Dam, the second one Matt's mom had mentioned, hold? What would happen if a wave of water headed toward Reno? Would it make it as far as Silver Valley?

Matt had to get home fast. And the peak of Howler's would have to wait for another day.

He gripped the rock and held on for dear life as his heart pounded against his ribs. He took short, sharp breaths. He knew his mom was in the business of rescuing people, and she would be smart and careful—but what if the water had surprised her? And what about his sister? Where was Bridget? Had she mentioned where she was meeting her friends? Matt tried to remember.

His phone started going crazy in his back pocket. It buzzed and dinged and pinged as text messages and voice mails came in one after the other. But Matt felt too light-headed to take his hands off the rock and answer it.

He had to get down. He had to get home to make sure his sister was okay. He had to reach his mom.

He wanted to jump down, but he needed to descend slowly and carefully—just like he'd climbed up. He waited until he felt calm enough to make his way back to solid ground.

Scout was waiting impatiently for him at the bottom. The dog was pacing and skittering across the dirt and still howling. He sounded frantic, like he couldn't wait to get back to base either.

"That's what you were so upset about," Matt said. "You knew what was happening, huh, Scout?"

Matt pulled his phone out of his pocket and quickly scanned the dozens of notifications. There were voice mails and texts from his mom, all of which basically said the same thing: *The first dam is going. The second might hold, but get to higher ground just in case.*

And there were several from his sister that said *MEET ME AT HOME NOW.*

Emergency air sirens blared in the city as Matt pedaled faster than he ever had in his life. Scout streaked along at his side, his paws barely touching the ground as he ran. With every stride, Scout's legs tucked underneath him, then stretched out again, driving him forward. His tongue dangled from the side of his mouth, and his ears pressed back against his head. He was more machine than animal, his grace and strength on full display as he ran.

They reached the base and zipped past the guard gate. There was no one there to stop them.

Matt and Scout reached the house within seconds. Matt flung open the door and they hurtled through it at top speed.

"Bridget!" Matt screamed. "Bridget! Where are you? We have to get out of here!"

He flew up the stairs.

Her bedroom was empty. She wasn't there.

Desperate, Matt looked out the window, hoping to see her in the backyard.

No one.

From his spot on the second floor, Matt had a wide view of the rest of the base, and the streets spreading out beyond it. What he saw made his blood run cold: The water was coming.

It was a flash flood.

Water filled the streets, swallowing driveways, setting off car alarms, and washing over speed bumps. It sent people running and screaming into their homes. And it was headed straight toward Matt's house.

Matt ran into his parents' bedroom to look in a different direction.

The streets on every side had become rivers. They were awash with water, several feet high, churning and chugging toward their house, carrying bikes and mailboxes and garbage cans in its foaming grasp.

He watched as the water knocked down his fence

and rushed through his yard. It slammed into the house. The walls shook, and Matt heard a series of explosive pops as the first-floor windows blew out. He heard water sloshing at the bottom of the stairs. He heard the furniture banging into the walls as the water carried it on its surge. The lights went out.

Matt and Scout ran into the upstairs hallway. Matt peered down the stairs. The water was as high as the middle stair, but it seemed to have stopped rising. For the moment.

Matt felt sick to his stomach, but also electrified and alert, like he'd had a thousand energy drinks.

His phone dinged in his pocket. Frantic, he swiped at it and read his sister's message: *Can't get home.*

Where are you? he typed back quickly. But the message wouldn't send. The phones had gone out. He had no idea where Bridget was.

It felt like the air was being squeezed out of Matt's lungs. Somehow he remembered to breathe, and he sucked in a deep gulp of oxygen.

A million thoughts crashed into each other in Matt's brain, but two rose up from the rest.

His sister was out there in the flood.

And he had to find her.

Matt dug through his parents' closet and found his dad's waders. They were the kind with built-in boots and straps that went over the shoulders—and they were huge. Matt knotted the straps to make them shorter. He layered on three pairs of socks and climbed into the waders. They were oversize, but they would do the trick.

Scout watched Matt get suited up. He hopped around and ran toward the bedroom door, then back to Matt, then back to the door again. Something about Scout's body language had changed, Matt could tell. He wasn't soft and happy, or jittery and vigilant.

This time, Scout was jazzed but focused. He was, Matt realized, in work mode.

Scout was ready to help.

"Let's go find Bridget, okay, Scout?" Matt said to the dog.

Scout wagged his tail.

Matt trudged down the hall. He passed his sister's closed door, and a mix of fear and sadness welled up in him. What if she was in real danger out there? What if he didn't find her fast enough?

Matt couldn't say what made him open her door, but he did. He just wanted to look inside, at her things.

He stepped in. Two textbooks lay open on the desk. Pens, notecards, and a calculator were scattered around nearby. A pile of laundry had grown tall in the corner. Her bed was hastily made.

He looked around, desperate for any kind of clue, any hint at all, to how he might find her.

His eyes fell on a crumpled pile of fabric on top of her pillow. It was a familiar faded gray, so old and threadbare that it was practically transparent. It was their dad's old T-shirt. The one she slept in every night while their dad was deployed.

He walked over to the bed and ran his fingers over the thin fabric. Without thinking, he picked it up and stuffed it in his backpack. Matt wasn't much of a believer in good-luck charms, but it certainly wasn't going to hurt.

He turned and left the room. Scout dashed ahead of him and stopped at the top of the stairs. The dog looked down at the dark water that had filled the first floor, then looked back at Matt, waiting for a command.

"Okay, Scout." A strange calm settled over Matt. The world around him had turned upside down—his living room churned like the bottom of the sea, everything as far as he could see was underwater, and he was separated from everyone in his family—but Matt felt entirely in control.

He pictured exactly what he was going to do before he did it.

He and Scout would go downstairs and get to the garage, swimming if they had to. They would climb up on his dad's jeep so Matt could reach the kayak hanging high up on the wall. And then they would climb into it, and Matt would paddle them out into the wild unknown outside so they could find his sister.

12

MATT'S BRAIN COULD BARELY COMPREHEND what he was seeing. These were the familiar streets of his neighborhood. There was the gas station and the movie theater and the ice-cream shop. But everything was underwater. Water carried bikes and scooters and flower boxes past the buildings and gas pumps. Water lapped at the windows of the pharmacy.

And instead of walking or biking down the street, Matt was paddling. He and Scout rode in the kayak down the middle of the road. Scout stood on the bow of the long, narrow craft, sniffing at the damp air around them, while Matt paddled as quickly as he could. The water was no longer a wild flood, but it had a current, and it was still rising. Matt could see it creeping up higher on the houses.

Scout was just as confused by what he was seeing and smelling. The water had thrown off his senses, and he was recalibrating. Matt could see from Scout's stance—from his flexed muscles and the tail poking straight up and curling around like a question mark— that the dog was on high alert.

Matt wished he knew more about Bridget's friends and where she could have gone. He knew she had gone to a study group, but other than that he had no idea where to start looking—so the answer was to look everywhere.

They turned onto a residential street, and Matt saw dozens of people sitting on their rooftops. Mothers and fathers hugged their children close, holding them back from the edge. Frantic dogs skittered back and forth across the shingles. Everyone had dazed looks on their faces.

They couldn't believe their eyes any more than Matt could. People waved at Matt as he rode by, and he waved back, but the whole scene was strangely quiet. Everyone was too stunned to speak. And if they could speak, what was there to say?

But where were the rescue crews, and where was his mom? Matt pushed away the worst thought: that his mom and her troops had been trapped by the flash flood. He pulled out his phone to try to text her, but his message still wouldn't deliver. With the power blown out, phone lines down, and water inundating cables and cell towers, it'd be a long time before service was back up and running.

Matt wasn't sure which way to go, so he steered the kayak toward the center of town. As he paddled, unanswered questions continued to gnaw at him. How far had his sister gotten before the dam broke? Had she been on the street or indoors when the water had hit? Would he and Scout be able to get very far in the kayak, or would it be too dangerous—or would there be too much damage—for them to continue?

Everywhere Matt looked, he saw more destruction. The first floor of every house he passed was flooded and totally destroyed. Fallen trees lay where they had crashed down onto garage roofs. Parked cars were underwater up to their windshields.

Scout moved around on the front of the boat, which dipped sharply left and right under his weight.

"Whoa, Scout!" Matt said. "Careful."

Scout didn't seem to hear him. He was sniffing frantically at the air around them, his snout bobbing up and down.

"What is it, buddy?" Matt asked, looking around and trying to see what Scout saw—or, more likely, saw and heard and smelled all at once.

Scout's eyes settled on a spot off to the left, about fifty yards ahead. He extended his head and his weight shifted forward. Matt leaned back to balance out the boat.

Matt paddled quickly and heard a faint cry coming from the spot Scout had homed in on. Matt picked up speed. The voice was louder and clearer now. It was coming from the left side of the road.

"Help!" It was a man. He was in the water, kicking and sputtering and flailing his arms. He was trying to swim across the road, toward an SUV to Matt's right, but the current was too strong. "I can't get across!" he cried in a desperate voice.

He spun around and frantically splashed his way back to a wide, heavy Dumpster just a few feet behind him. He grabbed hold of it and pulled himself on top, falling onto his stomach. The Dumpster rocked under his weight. He staggered to his feet unsteadily. Water lapped at his ankles as he stood on top of the large metal bin.

"Help me!" he screamed at Matt and Scout, waving his arms above his head. "Please! Help me! My daughter—my little girl—she's in there!" The man pointed back to the SUV across the road. The water had reached the bottom of the car's windows, and the windows were open. Matt could hear the scared cries of a young child from inside the car.

"Daddy! Where are you, Daddy?" the girl sobbed.

"It's okay, Sophie! Daddy's right here! I'm coming," the man called to his daughter. He turned to Matt, his face a mask of fear. "Please! Can you get my baby? Please help me!"

"We got her!" Matt shouted back. "It's okay! Sit down—please. Be careful." He plunged the paddle into the water and steered the kayak sharply to the right, toward the SUV. He paddled hard, moving across the strong, rough current.

Matt had been kayaking since he was a young boy. He could maneuver a boat in any kind of water, and he knew just how to place a paddle and redirect the kayak to keep moving.

Scout leaned over the front of the boat, his front

paws practically hanging off the edge. They got close to the car, but just as Matt reached out to grab the roof rack, the current pushed them along and rushed them past the vehicle. Matt paddled hard against the water to spin them around and get back to the car. It felt like a bad dream he often had, where he was running as hard and fast as he could but only moved an inch.

"Daddy!" Sophie screamed from inside the car.

Matt drove the paddle into the water over and over. Slowly, inch by inch, the kayak moved upstream and closer to the SUV. Matt stuck the paddle through the front window and lodged it against the steering wheel, steadying the boat. He held on to the other end with both hands.

Scout lowered his head and stuck it through the back window. Sophie cried out in surprise.

"Sophie!" Matt leaned in and locked eyes with the girl strapped into her car seat. She couldn't have been more than two or three years old. Water covered her lap. Her eyes were puffy and red, and her cheeks were blotchy from crying. "Hi." He tried to sound calm, like this wasn't a big deal. "I'm Matt, and this is Scout." Sophie sniffled.

"He's a really nice dog, okay?" Matt said. "And we're

going to help you. We're going to get you out of this car. Can you get out of your seat and climb onto the boat?"

Sophie shook her head through her tears. She pointed at the straps pulled tightly over her shoulders and across her waist. She was hooked in tight—and the buckles were underwater. Matt knew there was no way she'd be able to free herself.

He maneuvered the paddle against the steering wheel, trying to shift the position of the kayak so he could reach her. He took one hand off the paddle and stretched toward her as far as he could. But his hand on the paddle slipped, and the current caught the boat and started to pull it downstream, away from the car.

Matt clung to the paddle with one hand and grabbed on to the doorframe with the other, just in time to stop the kayak from getting away. He eased it back toward the car. Now he had one hand on the car and one on the end of the paddle, and it wasn't safe to let go of either.

Matt realized he wasn't going to be able to reach Sophie.

Scout would have to do it.

"Scout," Matt said. Scout's ears flicked at the sound

of Matt's voice. He seemed to understand what he had to do. "Go." Scout wagged his tail at the command. He was ready to go.

As Matt held the boat steady, Scout climbed over and put one front paw, then the other, onto the window frame of the girl's door. The boat rocked under his back legs. Matt did his best to steady it. "Scout, in," Matt directed, hoping Scout would understand what he meant. It seemed to work. When the balance was just right, Scout clambered quickly through the open window, into the car.

Sophie stopped crying and reached out a hand to pet him on the head. Scout licked water off her nose, and she smiled weakly through her tears.

"Attaboy, Scout," Matt said. "Sophie, sit still and Scout will get you out of there." She nodded and sniffled.

"Scout, can you chew through the straps?" Matt asked the dog. Scout gave him a confused look, his ears perked up.

"Scout, chew," Matt said again. He gestured at his own shoulders and pointed at Sophie.

Scout turned back to Sophie. He nosed around the girl's shoulders and neck, and she giggled. To Matt's amazement, Scout gently took the strap over her right shoulder in his teeth. The harness pulled tight across Sophie's chest, and she let out a small cry. "Don't worry, Sophie—Scout's not going to bite you. He just wants to chew the strap of your car seat, okay?"

She nodded, but her face screwed up into a petrified expression, and she started to cry again.

"No, no, no, Sophie!" Matt tried to sound as soothing as he could. "Really, he's not going to hurt you. He wants to help you, I promise. Look at me. Just look over here right at me."

Her tearstained face turned to Matt.

"Keep your eyes on me. Do you have a doggie like mine?"

She shook her head.

"No? What about a kitty?"

She nodded.

"You have a cat!" Matt exhaled, relieved to have something—anything—he could work with. "What's your cat's name?"

"Pudding."

"Pudding? That's a great name for a cat. Let me guess—you named him, right?"

Sophie nodded and a grin spread across her face.

Scout was gnawing and tugging on the tight strap. She flinched every time it dug into her neck or Scout's teeth brushed against her skin. Matt could tell that Scout was making progress—the stretch of thick nylon was starting to fray and come apart. Matt just needed to keep Sophie distracted.

"Is she chocolate pudding? Or is she more like vanilla pudding?"

"Butterscotch!" Sophie squealed.

"That's my favorite pudding," Matt said.

Scout's top lip curled up as he worked.

Hurry up, Scout, Matt thought.

Finally, with a *pop*, the last threads of the strap broke and Sophie's right shoulder was free. Scout stepped across her lap and started chewing on the left strap. His body crossed over hers, and Sophie leaned down and rubbed her chin across the soft fur on the back of Scout's neck. She wrapped her arms around his chest and gave him a big hug. Scout stopped chewing for a second and gave her one good lick on the ear, then resumed his work.

After a few minutes, the second strap broke free. There was still a belt over her lap, but she could pull herself out of it.

"Good work, Scout!" Matt said. "Sophie—can you pull yourself up and out of your car seat?"

"No," she said, her eyes growing big and round with fear. She pointed to her upper arm. "Need floaties!"

She was scared to get out of her seat and into the water.

"Oh, no—you won't have to swim! You can just climb out of the car and right onto this boat, okay?"

She stared at him.

"I just need you to stand up out of your seat like . . . like you're getting up to go to the park with your dad. Can you do that for me?"

She nodded, but she didn't look so sure.

"Stand up!"

Sophie stiffened her body and straightened her legs but stayed in her seat.

Scout jammed his nose under her armpit and nudged upward. She scrunched up her face and shook her head from side to side. Scout repeated his gesture. He looked up at her, his face just a couple of inches from hers. She looked him right in the eye.

"Okay, Scout," she said. "I get up."

Sophie wriggled out of the belt across her lap and climbed out of her seat. She waded through the water in the back seat and leaned out the window. Matt steadied the kayak against the car.

"Just climb on board, Sophie," he said gently. "Just like you're climbing onto the jungle gym."

Scout followed closely behind her and, as she reached her hands out to the slippery kayak, he gripped her shirt with his teeth. He wasn't going to let her fall into the water and get swept away.

Sophie scrambled onto the front of the kayak and crawled on her hands and knees toward Matt.

"You did it!" Matt cried. "Great job! Sit down, Sophie, and we'll go get your dad."

Scout emerged from the car and took his position on the bow. Matt waited until Scout was settled and slid the paddle out from the steering wheel.

The current picked up the kayak, and they began to float away.

13

MATT PADDLED HARD ACROSS THE RAGING stream that filled the street, making his way toward Sophie's dad. Matt had barely pulled the boat against the Dumpster when the man reached out and wrapped Sophie in a tight hug.

"Hi, Daddy," Sophie said into her dad's shoulder.

"Hi, baby." He turned to Matt and Scout. "Thank you," he whispered to them. "Thank you for saving her."

"Scout did all the work," Matt said, tipping his head toward the dog. "Climb in," he said to the man. "We'll get you somewhere safe."

Sophie scooted over and her dad eased himself into the kayak. He sat down and pulled Sophie into his lap, squeezing her tightly, like he was never going to let go again. Sophie wriggled in his grip.

Matt let go of the Dumpster and the kayak coasted along on the current for a moment. Blisters were forming on his fingers and palms, and his arms were shaking from exertion. He shook out his hands and rolled his shoulders a couple of times. He wiped the sweat from his brow with his sleeve.

Matt began to paddle again, but he wasn't sure where to take Sophie and her dad to make sure they'd stay safe. And he still needed to find Bridget. He surveyed the scene around them. As far as the eye could see, the streets were flooded and buildings were destroyed. The only people he saw were on rooftops and standing on their cars—and there was still no help in sight.

It was disaster everywhere he looked.

Their town looked like another planet.

Matt steered the kayak toward a short strip of stores at the center of town.

No one spoke as he paddled. Scout lay on the bow like a sentry, his head and ears up and his eyes taking in everything around them. His head turned and his ears flicked at any sound—a baby's muffled cry, a tree branch scraping against the top of a car.

Matt was so proud of the way Scout had acted back there. He had been smart enough to figure out how to save Sophie, and now Matt was even more convinced that he was a pretty amazing dog. If only his mom could have seen it.

Matt felt his paddle knock into something hard. He looked over the side of the boat and made out asphalt a couple of feet underwater. They had reached higher ground. Ahead of them, he saw the supermarket where he and his sister had gone shopping just a few days earlier. The building was set up on a low hill, which meant its parking lot was mostly above the waterline.

They drifted closer, and Sophie's dad let out a cry of relief when they could see around the far side of the building. Several dozen people huddled together in the parking lot, close to the store's front door. They were soaking wet, their pants clinging to their legs and their hair plastered to their faces. They wore pained, shell-shocked expressions. They clustered together for comfort.

Matt had never been so glad to see such a bunch of bedraggled-looking people in his life. He scanned the crowd for the familiar form of his sister.

"Over here!" a man called to them from the lot, waving his arms in the air. "Paddle over here!"

Matt paddled hard on the left side of the boat, slowly moving the boat to the right. They cruised toward the parking lot, stopping only when the bottom of the kayak scraped against the pavement. Scout scuttled across the bow and sat down at Sophie's knee.

"Hi," the girl said, reaching out to pat him on the head.

"I'll hold the boat steady," Matt said to Sophie's dad. "You climb out first." He nodded. Matt braced the paddle against the ground. Scout put his head on Sophie's lap, and she giggled.

Sophie's dad carefully hoisted himself out of the boat and into the shallow water. The boat wobbled from side to side, but Matt managed to keep it steady. Sophie's dad reached back over the side and lifted his daughter under the armpits, easing her out of the boat.

"Come on, baby," he cooed at her. "I got you."

Sophie dropped her head onto her dad's shoulder. Her whole body relaxed as she sagged in his arms. Sophie's dad turned back to Matt and mouthed *Thank you* again. Matt nodded. The man waded through the water and onto dry land.

Matt hopped out too and dragged the kayak around the side of the building, to a dry spot in the parking lot. Scout followed Matt toward the group of stunned, frightened people. He heard snippets of conversation—"Help is coming," "What are we going to do now?" and "How could this happen?"—as he bobbed through the crowd, searching for his sister. He looked at every single person once, twice. He asked every one of them if they'd seen a girl by Bridget's description.

No one had.

Matt felt himself getting more and more nervous with every person he asked.

When he got to the outer edge of the crowd, Matt peered into the little alleyway behind the building to see if anyone was there. It was empty. He turned around and made his way back through the group again.

Bridget was nowhere to be seen.

"Scout, come!" Matt said, heading back toward the kayak. They would just have to keep going until they found her. Every second they stayed in the parking lot was another second Bridget was out there by herself. A sense of urgency bordering on panic filled Matt's whole body. Scout trotted along by his side but suddenly stopped to sniff something on the ground. Matt kept moving but turned his head to see what the dog had found—and crashed headlong into someone coming the other way.

"Sorry!" Matt said, raising his hands toward the soaking-wet person he had just walked into.

"No worries, Matt," a familiar voice said. "Dude—can you believe this?"

It was Dev. He had just arrived at the grocery store, trailed by a crew of friends sloshing through the water behind him. Their faces were pale and drawn.

"No," Matt said, shaking his head. "It's awful. Glad you're okay."

"We came to find their parents," Dev said, jerking a thumb toward his friends. At just that moment, several adults broke free from the crowd and, with cries of joy and relief, ran to the kids, their arms open wide.

"Are your parents here too?"

Dev shook his head. "They're safe at their office. I talked to them before service went down."

"That's great," Matt said. But he couldn't stay and chat—he had to keep moving. "I have to go—I'll see you later. You guys will be safe here."

"Go?" Dev asked, surprised. "Where? The cops are telling everyone to get here and stay here." He looked over Matt's shoulder at the assembled group.

"I have to find Bridget—my sister. She couldn't get home in time, so she's . . ." Matt trailed off. He felt queasy just thinking about all the possible endings that sentence could have.

Dev waited for Matt to finish, but before Matt could speak, a loud rumble interrupted them. All heads turned toward the street—or what until recently had been a street but was now a fast-moving waterway.

Several large vehicles headed straight toward them, plowing through the water like battleships. They had the hull of a boat, but they moved and sounded like trucks; Matt's ears vibrated with the thrumming of their engines.

The crowd gasped as the vehicles turned in to the parking lot and emerged from the water like giant robots in a sci-fi movie, crunching forward on tank wheels. Matt had seen these amphibious vehicles around the military bases his parents had worked on over the years. They were designed for just this kind of situation.

The vehicles had barely lurched to a stop when women and men in uniform streamed out of them, rushing toward the people by the store. The troops called out commands and began a head count.

These were soldiers from Matt's mom's command. His heart lurched in his chest. Was his mom here? He desperately wanted to know that she was okay, but he didn't want her to know that Bridget was missing—it wouldn't be right to worry her about her own daughter when she had so many other people to help. Matt just needed a chance to find Bridget.

But if his mom's soldiers saw him, they would never let him leave.

He had to get out of there fast.

Matt looked over at his kayak, but it was across the parking lot, in plain sight. If he headed for it, he would be seen—and stopped—instantly. He looked around frantically, trying to find an alternate route.

He remembered something his dad had always told him about his military training—although Matt had mostly used the advice in high-stakes games of hide-and-seek: *People don't always see what's right in front of them.*

"Gotta go." Matt took off, diving back into the cluster of people gathered by the store.

"Wait—" Dev started to say.

But Matt ignored him. "Scout, come!"

With the dog following close behind him, Matt

used the crowd as cover. He weaved quickly through the throng, making his way down the side of the building. If his plan worked, he would just be one more person in a sea of people, and no one would notice him.

They reached the back corner of the building. Matt took a quick look over his shoulder to make sure no one was watching. The plan had worked. Everyone was preoccupied, and not a single person was looking their way.

Matt and Scout slipped around behind the building and down the alleyway, where the troops couldn't see them. They would go the long way around the building to get to the kayak.

"Matt—what are you doing?"

Matt jumped at the sound of his friend's voice. He turned around and found Dev fast on their heels. Matt shot him a silencing look and held a finger to his lips.

Matt and Scout kept moving, and Dev kept following. They made their way around the building and soon slowed to a stop. They had reached the front corner of the grocery store.

One more step, and they would be in full view of the National Guard.

Carefully, Matt peeked his head out from behind the building and took stock of the situation. He eyed his kayak about ten feet straight ahead. Off to his left, he saw the soldiers spreading out, setting up floodlights and tents across the parking lot. Several of them had clipboards and were moving from person to person— probably taking names.

"Matt," Dev said, "it's really not safe for you to go out on the water."

"Scout and I will be fine." Matt kept his eyes on the troops, waiting for just the right moment to run for his kayak.

He saw his chance.

Matt took a deep breath. "Scout, come!" he said as he shot out from behind the building and raced toward the boat.

Once again, Dev was right behind him.

"I'm coming with you," Dev said. "I'll help you find her."

"No—Dev—seriously, stay here." Matt grabbed hold of the kayak and began dragging it down the slope toward the water. Scout trotted along beside him, anxious to get up on the bow again. The sound of the kayak scraping along the asphalt rang loudly in Matt's ears. He winced, and crossed his fingers that no one else would hear it.

"It'll be faster if we trade off paddling, right?" Dev said. "Just let me help." He leaned down and grabbed the other side of the kayak.

Matt was surprised by his new friend's persistence. The truth was, he wouldn't mind Dev's company. In an instant, the world had become a giant watery mess, and Matt had no idea what kind of chaos—or danger—he was heading into. Two heads—and sets of hands—were better than one.

But that was also exactly why he didn't want Dev to come.

If anything happened to him, it would be all Matt's fault.

"I'm pretty fast on my own," Matt insisted, sounding more confident than he felt.

"Fine," Dev shot back, "but I know my way around town better than you do. If you get lost, it's just going to slow you down."

Matt opened his mouth to say something, but no words came out. He couldn't argue with Dev on that one.

Dev was right. Matt needed his help.

Matt would just have to make sure nothing happened to him.

"Fine," Matt said. "But only if you can keep up." They had reached the water's edge, and the kayak was starting to float. So far no one had spotted them.

Matt splashed in, knee-deep. As soon as the boat was fully afloat, he sat on it sideways, swung his legs around toward the front, and picked up a paddle. Scout took three running strides into the water and leaped upward in a graceful arc, landing smoothly on the back of the kayak. He scrambled past Matt and took up his position on the bow again.

Matt held the paddle in the air, poised for launch. He looked back at Dev, who was slogging through the water toward them, his jeans soaked all the way up to his thighs. "You coming?" Matt asked.

Dev grabbed on to the side of the boat, threw a leg over it, and clambered aboard. He folded himself onto the tiny seat in front of Matt. "Let's go."

The kayak dipped lower in the water under Dev's weight. Matt plunged the paddle underwater and pushed off against the ground to get some momentum. He paddled hard until he felt the front of the boat cross into the current, which pulled them in. Just as the water began to carry them swiftly along, a loud chorus of shouts echoed from the parking lot behind them.

"Hey!"

"Get back here!"

"Boys, you need to stay here—it's not safe out there!"

And then, through a megaphone: "This is Sergeant Lopez with the National Guard. Come back onto land. I repeat: Come back onto land."

At the sound of the booming voice, Scout stood up on the bow and looked back at the parking lot, his head and tail held high. Matt and Dev looked over their shoulders at the crowd, then back at each other.

Dev nodded at Matt. Matt nodded at Dev.

"Paddle!" Dev cried.

Matt paddled. They rode the current, and they were gone.

14

"LET ME TAKE OVER." DEV REACHED for the paddle after Matt had been going at it for a while. Matt was more than happy to oblige. His arms were shaking, and his hands were stiff. He decided then and there that he was happy to have Dev along for the search.

He handed over the paddle and opened and closed his fingers a few times to get the blood flowing again.

"Where was your sister before the flood?" Dev asked.

"I don't know." Matt's voice broke. "She just said she was meeting some friends. She was going to a study group."

A wave of despair threatened to crash down on

Matt. He buried his face in his hands and wished there were some way—any way—to know where Bridget could be. But feeling hopeless wasn't going to help him find her any faster.

"So, maybe the library?" Dev offered.

Matt looked up. "Yeah," he said, relieved to have a place to start. "Good idea."

"Let's try it." Dev steered the boat to the right, down a side street. "It's not too far from school."

While Dev paddled, Matt checked his phone. The text he'd tried to send Bridget was still unsent. Cell phone service was still down.

If she wasn't at the library, there would literally be no way to track her down.

"What's up with Scout?" Dev asked.

Matt raised his head. Scout was staring at him from the front of the kayak, like he wanted something. The dog looked away and started moving back and forth across the narrow space, sniffing at the air.

"Whoa!" Dev steadied the boat as it rocked under Scout's shifting weight.

And that's when Matt realized that he *did* have a way to find his sister—a highly trained, very effective way.

Scout.

He unzipped the backpack at his feet. The T-shirt his sister wore every night—their dad's old one—was right at the top. He pulled it out and held it on his lap for a second, feeling the worn, soft fabric under his palms.

"Scout, come."

Scout stepped carefully into the seating area. He slipped past Dev and sat down on top of Matt's feet.

He held the cloth out to the dog. Scout buried his snout in the shirt, sniffed a few times, moved his nose around, then exhaled sharply, as if he was clearing out his nostrils. He repeated the process a few more times—sniffing, nudging at the cloth, exhaling.

Dev stopped paddling and watched them. "Is that your sister's shirt?" he asked.

Matt nodded. "I think maybe Scout can track her."

"Using her scent, you mean?"

"Yeah."

"That would be insane."

Matt agreed, but he didn't know what other choice they had.

They sat in silence for a couple of minutes while the boat drifted along. Scout pulled his head out of the T-shirt and looked up at Matt.

His eyes glinted in the sunlight. His tail wagged. He was ready.

Matt wasn't sure what to do next. How would he know if Scout was tracking his sister's scent? How would Scout tell him which way to go? But there was only one way to find out, and that was by doing it.

"Scout, search!" Matt figured that was as good a command as any. "Go ahead and start paddling," he told Dev. "Let's see if he can tell us which way to go."

Dev picked up the paddle and began steering them toward the town library. Scout resumed his position on the bow of the kayak, leaning into his front legs, every muscle in his body flexed and primed. He sniffed at the air in front of him, then to his left and right, then back again.

After a few minutes, Dev stopped paddling. Matt looked around and saw that they were just a couple of blocks from their school.

"Dude, he's not doing anything," Dev said.

"We just have to give him a chance," Matt said, hoping he was right.

They floated into the middle of a four-way inter-section. A traffic light dangled above them but, like everything else in town, it had gone totally dark.

"Which way, Scout?" Matt asked.

Scout just stared at him.

Matt had an idea. "Start paddling," he said to Dev. He kept his gaze on Scout, hoping the dog would give him some kind of signal, some kind of clue.

With a grunt, Dev dug the paddle into the water and got them moving again. There were four directions they could head in. "Talk to me, Scout," Dev said.

Still nothing.

"Go left," Matt suggested. "Let's see what happens."

Dev steered the boat down the street to their left. Scout jumped up and started barking loudly and intensely, looking back over his shoulder at Matt.

"I think he's saying that's not the right way," Matt said, going on a hunch.

Dev dipped the paddle into the water and steered them back to the intersection. Scout stopped barking.

Dev redirected them toward the next street to the right. Again, Scout let out a loud series of sharp barks, as if he was trying to tell them something.

"Nope," Dev said, turning the boat around and paddling them back to the crossroads.

"Third time's a charm," Matt said. *Wishful thinking,* he thought.

Dev guided the kayak down a third street. "This is the way to the library," he said over his shoulder.

Scout sat down.

"What's he doing? Is he stopping?" Dev asked.

Matt studied the dog's body language for a moment: He wasn't relaxed. He wasn't sitting down because he was tired. Scout's muscles were still tensed, his ears were up, and his eyes were alert.

Matt thought back to the dog he had seen in training at his mom's K-9 facility. As soon as she had found the baseball cap, she'd sat down and waited for her handler.

That was the signal.

Scout was telling Matt he had found Bridget's scent. They continued down the street, which passed right in front of their school on the way to the library. Scout didn't bark. He sat on the bow with his head held high, calmly sniffing at the air.

"I think this is it," Matt said. "He's not barking, anyway."

As they got closer to their school, Scout's head began swiveling around in all directions. His whiskers quivered.

About a quarter of a mile down the road, they

floated into the school parking lot. Matt looked up at the building, and for a second he couldn't understand what he was seeing.

The first floor of their school was totally submerged under the floodwaters.

The second floor was just barely above the waterline.

"Wow." Dev let out a long, low whistle in disbelief and paddled them closer to the dark building. Scout stood up and sniffed at the air.

A chill went through Matt as he tried to take it all in. Just forty-eight hours earlier, their school was teeming with life. Now it was underwater, isolated—an island in the middle of a changed landscape.

Suddenly, Scout's head shot up, and he stared intently at the building. His ears flicked forward, and his eyebrows went up.

He had heard something.

And then Matt heard it too. It was faint at first, but then it grew loud and clear: There was someone calling for help.

Someone was trapped inside the school.

Matt scanned the front of the building but didn't see anyone. The windows were still.

"Help!"

Scout whimpered as his head swiveled toward the sound.

It was coming from the other side of the building.

Dev paddled them around the school as quickly as he could. He steadied the kayak, holding them in one spot. Matt held his breath as he ran his eyes across the building, but he still couldn't see anyone.

Scout whined and barked and scratched at the thick plastic surface of the kayak with his front paws. He was anxious to get out and help—but who could he help? And where?

"Help! Someone, please!"

"There!" Matt pointed up at a small open window on the very end of the building. A girl leaned out over the windowsill.

She looked familiar. Matt squinted into the distance, trying to make out her face.

It was Amaiya.

She looked around frantically, not spotting them right away.

"Is anyone there?" she cried out. Her voice was strained and scared, as if she had no real expectation of a reply.

"Amaiya—we're here!" Matt and Dev shouted at the same time, their voices echoing off the building.

Amaiya followed the sound of their voices until she spotted the kayak, Scout, and the boys. Her face lit up.

"Dev? Matt?" she choked out, her voice breaking with emotion and relief. "Please—can you help me? I can't get out of here!"

"We're coming!" Matt called back. "Just stay there."

Dev paddled toward the school, but they had only gone a few feet when the boat slammed into something dark and heavy bobbing on the surface. The kayak lurched sideways. Matt and Dev grabbed on to keep from flying out of it, and Scout scrabbled sideways on the bow.

"What was that?" Matt asked.

Dev leaned down and peered at the water. "A Dumpster." The massive metal bin was practically invisible as it floated in the dark water. Dev steered the boat around it.

A field of debris had collected around the school building.

"Watch out—" Matt pointed at the trunk of a felled tree and a long, spiky section of chain-link fence that floated nearby.

"Got it." Dev focused hard as he navigated around the obstacles.

They pulled up close to the sand-colored walls of their school. The water lapped at the building. Matt looked up at Amaiya, who leaned out of the window several feet above them. Holding his arms out to his sides for balance, he stood up in the center of the kayak, steadying himself, while Dev used small, quick strokes to keep the boat in position. Scout scratched at the wall of the building with one paw.

"Hi," Matt called up to her.

"Hi," Amaiya replied. Her eyes were red and puffy from crying. "I can't believe you guys are here. Wait, why *are* you here?"

Matt shrugged. "We thought you might be hanging around."

Amaiya laughed, and Dev groaned.

"Help her get down, would you, dude?" Dev said. "I can't keep paddling like this forever."

"Why are *you* here?" Matt asked Amaiya.

"I was coming home from the library when the water"—her eyes welled up at the memory—"when I saw the water coming. I didn't know what to do, so I ran into the school. What if the door had been locked?" She choked back a sob. "Then the water started coming in, so I ran up to the second floor."

"You did great, Amaiya," Matt reassured her. "We're going to get you out of there—I promise. We just need a minute to figure out how." Matt looked down at Dev. "How are we going to get her out of there?" he asked under his breath.

"We can't reach that window," Dev replied grimly.

"And she can't jump in the water," Matt said. "It's too dangerous."

They searched the water around them for something they could use to help her down. There were large shards of broken wood, more chain-link fence, and a car bumper—but nothing useful.

Matt and Dev exchanged a glance. They both knew what the last remaining option was: Amaiya would have to jump onto the kayak. Hopefully the boat wouldn't flip over—or sink—when she landed.

Dev nodded at Matt, and Matt turned back to Amaiya.

"Here's what I want you to do," Matt called up to her. "I want you to hang out the window feetfirst and lower yourself down as far as you can go. And then you're just going to let go and drop the rest of the way. I'll catch you, okay?"

Amaiya shook her head. "Not okay."

"You're going to be fine."

"You can do this, Amaiya," Dev chimed in. "Come on."

"No—I'm scared."

Matt squeezed his eyes shut, trying not to let his frustration show. He understood how Amaiya felt—it was a scary situation—and he wasn't going anywhere until she was safe. But he was also very aware that every moment spent helping her was time he wasn't looking for his sister.

Matt felt pulled in too many directions at once. His mind was whirring, but he wasn't sure what to do next.

And then he heard his dad's voice again, repeating a favorite refrain: *Problems make you feel overwhelmed, Matt, but solutions make you feel powerful. Always focus on the solution, not the problem.*

His dad repeated this to Matt whenever he was struggling with something—whether it was a stubborn topic sentence or a fight with a friend. And the advice had never failed him.

While Amaiya clung to the window and Dev paddled quickly, Matt took a moment to think.

The solution he needed now was to get Amaiya out of the building so she would be safe—and so he could go find Bridget.

But Amaiya was too scared to jump out of the building, so the solution was to get her to overcome her fear.

And what was the best weapon against fear? Confidence.

How could Matt build Amaiya's confidence? They barely knew each other, but he had learned a few things about her already.

She was a great swimmer.

She was a great rock climber.

She wasn't afraid when she was scaling the boulders at the ravine, or even when she was climbing Howler's Peak.

Solutions make you feel powerful.

"Okay." Matt's voice was firm. "Amaiya, listen to me. I saw you climbing Howler's yesterday. Right?"

She nodded.

"Were you scared when you climbed it?"

She shook her head.

"You weren't scared, but Howler's is really hard to climb, right? I tried it—and you saw how that ended."

She laughed. "I did."

"So I know this is kind of an insane situation. I mean"—Matt waved an arm at the watery scene around them—"our school is underwater. Our town is underwater. You're trapped on the second floor, and we're being stalked by a floating Dumpster. It's all super weird."

"It's so super weird." She nodded.

"But you're still you, right?"

She looked confused. "What? I mean—I guess so."

"And *you* can climb Howler's, which is way harder than getting out of that window. Take my word for it."

She sucked in her breath and considered his words.

"So," Matt finished, "if you can do that, then you can definitely do this."

"Nice," Dev whispered to Matt.

Amaiya leaned farther out the window and looked straight down at the kayak and the water below. She looked up and out toward the horizon, at the water that stretched as far as she could see.

And then she made up her mind.

Like an Olympic diver preparing to jump, Amaiya

exhaled slowly through her mouth and shook out her arms. Gripping the sides of the window frame tightly, she threw one leg over the windowsill, then the other, and scooted forward until her legs dangled against the building. She sat like that for a moment, totally still.

"Scout, lie down," Matt said. Scout followed the command. Dev steadied the boat and kept them as close to the wall as possible. Matt planted his feet as firmly as he could and bent his knees a little. He reached his hands up to her and nodded.

No one spoke.

Amaiya closed her eyes. She slowly turned her body around and, gripping the windowsill tightly with her hands, lowered herself down until she was hanging by her arms. She faced the building and couldn't see Matt below her.

"On three, okay?" he said.

"Okay." Her voice was muffled.

"One. Two. Three."

Amaiya let go. She dropped straight down toward the kayak—and Matt's outstretched arms.

His hands closed around her waist and her trajectory slowed as she slammed into him. They both stumbled and sat down, hard, on the stern.

The back half of the kayak sank a few inches underwater.

"Whoa!" Matt yelled. "There's too much weight back here! Amaiya—quick—move forward!"

Amaiya scrambled to her knees, but before she had a chance to shift her weight toward the middle of the boat, something heavy in the water whacked into them from the left. The kayak smashed into the side of the building. Amaiya fell onto her side.

Matt gripped the edges of the kayak to keep from flying off. The water was up around his waist. "Ow!" he cried as a sharp point of chain link scratched at his knee.

Finally, Amaiya regained her balance and scooted to the middle of the boat, at the same moment that Dev lurched forward onto the bow next to Scout, trying to add weight to the front.

At the back, Matt felt himself rising up out of the water—then up and up some more. Something was wrong—he was going too high.

They were too heavy in front, and the stern popped up into the air while the bow began to sink. Several inches of water sloshed around the center of the kayak.

They had taken on water.

Not only would they have to get the kayak balanced out, but they'd have to bail out the water as well.

"Dev!" Matt yelled.

Dev's eyes got huge as he quickly realized what was happening. He tried to correct and scramble back toward the middle, but as he did, he bumped his elbow hard on the side of the boat.

Matt watched in horror as the paddle flew out of Dev's hand and flipped through the air, as if in slow motion. Dev snapped his arm out to grab it, but it slipped through his fingers.

Dev froze. Matt froze. Amaiya gasped.

The paddle landed in the water ten feet away with a crisp *plunk!*

Matt and Dev exchanged a terrified look.

Do something, Matt commanded himself. But before he could think of just what that something might be, Scout stood up and, without a hint of hesitation, hurled himself off the bow and into the water.

"Scout, no!" Matt screamed. But Scout was already swimming hard toward the paddle, his front paws cutting the water, his head tipped back and his snout gliding above the surface. The dog expertly maneuvered around the debris cluttering his path, skirting the tree trunk and car bumper.

Scout drew close to the paddle, but every time he snatched at it with his teeth, it floated just beyond his reach, like it was being pulled by an invisible string. But Scout kept at it, a determined look in his eye.

Then Matt spotted something in the water that made his stomach churn.

Just a few feet away from the dog, a large, dark-green shape spun in the current.

The Dumpster.

Even empty, the giant metal bin was heavy. And it was headed straight for Scout.

"Look out!" Matt shouted. Scout's ears flicked at the sound of Matt's voice, but he kept his eyes on the paddle. There was nothing Matt could do but watch. Scout was on his own in the murky water.

Within seconds, the Dumpster slammed into Scout, whacking him hard on the head.

Scout disappeared beneath the surface.

"No!" Matt, Dev, and Amaiya screamed in unison.

Matt felt sick. He desperately watched the water,

waiting for a sign—any sign—of Scout.

Nothing.

Without stopping to think, Matt stripped off his dad's waders, ready to dive in after the dog.

"Wait!" Dev said.

"There!" Amaiya pointed.

Matt saw Scout's brown-and-white head pop up on the far side of the Dumpster. He was splashing back toward the paddle, his nostrils flaring as he breathed heavily from the exertion.

Scout was okay.

Matt let out a cry of relief and bent over with his hands on his knees. He took a couple of breaths to slow his speeding heart.

"Yes! He got it." Dev pumped a fist in the air.

Matt looked up to see Scout swimming back in their direction with the paddle lodged firmly in his jaw, his front legs chopping through the water.

Scout reached the kayak. Dev grabbed the paddle from his mouth while Amaiya and Matt hauled the dog aboard.

With one big shake, Scout dried himself off and showered the kids with water. His fur stuck out in every direction, like he'd been blow-dried. He plopped down on the bottom of the boat, licked more water off his coat, and, panting heavily, looked around at his three fellow passengers like it was just an ordinary day.

Matt, Dev, and Amaiya burst out laughing.

"That dog is amazing," Amaiya said.

"No kidding." Dev shook his head in disbelief.

Matt dropped to his knees and wrapped his arms around Scout's neck. "You really are," he said into the dog's wet fur.

Scout stuck his cold nose on Matt's cheek. He sniffed at Matt's ear, licked Matt's eyebrow, then dropped his head onto his paws, ready for a rest.

15

IT WAS MATT'S TURN TO PADDLE. They were all silent as the boat moved along quickly. It was already afternoon, and the sun was high in the sky. Matt wiped the sweat from his brow.

"You were right, Dev," Matt said after a few minutes.

"I'm sorry—what was that?"

"I said you were right—" Matt stopped talking and shook his head. Even under the circumstances, he couldn't fight a smile. "Oh. You heard me the first time, didn't you?"

"Yup." Dev chuckled. "I just really wanted to hear it again."

"I couldn't have done this alone."

"Nope."

They were quiet again.

Matt paddled toward the library. Scout lay on the pointed bow of the kayak, still a little dazed. He didn't look like he was ready to start leading the way again.

They reached the library within a few minutes. The building was dark and silent—abandoned-looking. It was set on a slight rise, with a grand staircase out front leading up to the main entrance. Most of the library was above the waterline, and a group of about a dozen people sat clustered together at the top of the stairs.

"Hey!" Matt called out. He steered the boat over toward them. His heart pounded in his chest as he anxiously scanned their shell-shocked faces.

Bridget wasn't with them. Matt was crushed.

The group called out a chorus of greetings and waved Matt and the others over.

"Are you guys okay?" Dev asked. Everyone nodded.

"We're all safe," an older woman said. "We're just waiting for help to come."

"The National Guard will be here soon," Dev replied. "We just saw them getting set up at the grocery store."

The people on the stairs let out a collective cheer.

"Um, excuse me . . ." Matt was almost afraid to ask. "I'm looking for my sister. I think she was supposed to be here. Her name is Bridget Tackett? She's seventeen and has long dark brown hair. She wears glasses?"

He looked from one to the other of them, hoping someone would recognize her name or description. They shook their heads apologetically.

"Tackett, you said?" It was the older lady.

"Yes!" Matt sat up straighter. "Did you see her?"

"She checked out a book from me right before the water hit."

"She did? Where is she? Is she still here?"

The woman's face fell. She hesitated, then said, "She left, sweetie. Right after she checked out."

Matt felt like someone had punched him in the gut. Amaiya put a hand on his arm, steadying him.

"She'll be fine," Amaiya said. "I made it to the school. I bet she made it somewhere safe too."

Matt nodded and buried his face in his hands. He wished he could believe her.

"Guys," Amaiya said to Matt and Dev, "I'm going to stay here."

Matt's head shot up. "What do you mean? Why?"

"You'll be able to move faster with fewer people.

Plus," she said, "you're going to need my spot when you find your sister."

Matt managed a weak smile. "Thanks," he said.

Matt paddled closer to the steps. Amaiya hopped off and waded through the water and up the stairs. People in the group scooted over, making room for her to sit with them. She settled into a spot between two little kids and their moms.

"Good luck," Amaiya said. "You're going to find her."

"I hope so," Matt replied. "But I'm glad we found you first."

Amaiya waved them off.

Matt steered the boat away from the library. He paddled a few fast strokes, and the kayak shot forward in a smooth motion, headed back toward the watery road. The people on the stairs grew small in the distance.

They were in a quiet stretch on the edge of town, where there were few houses or buildings.

"Where to?" Dev asked.

"That's up to Scout." Matt eyed the dog at the front of the boat. He knew Scout wasn't back to 100 percent.

But Scout was their only shot. Without him, they could paddle around for hours—days, even—and get no closer to finding Bridget.

Matt rested the paddle on his knees and pulled Bridget's T-shirt back out from his backpack. "Come on, buddy. Please—I know your head probably hurts, but can you tell us which way to go?" He held the shirt under Scout's muzzle. Scout looked at it but did nothing; he just panted.

"Please?" Matt begged. He held the T-shirt out again.

One second ticked by. Two seconds. Matt held his breath.

At last, Scout buried his nose in the shirt and snuffled around. Then he turned his head and stared downstream.

"What does that mean?" Dev asked.

Matt studied Scout. He seemed more attentive than he had been before. He sniffed the air, and the fur between his shoulders twitched. He seemed . . . ready.

"I think it means we're going in the right direction." Matt took up the paddle again and got them moving. "At least I hope so." Matt paused to lean forward and gently scratch behind Scout's ears. "Thanks, pal." Scout closed his eyes and relished the scratching for a second.

There were no further signs from Scout, other than his nose working hard. As Scout's nostrils flared, Matt knew that he was sorting through the thousands—even tens of thousands—of scents that Matt and Dev could never catch in a million years. And he knew that if Scout was able to find the one strand of scent that Bridget might have left behind, he would follow it until he dropped from exhaustion.

Dev took over the paddling duties, and Matt shook out his hands. He slipped his phone out of his pocket and checked it for the hundredth time. Still no signal. Not a single bar, not a single message coming in or going out. He had no idea where his mom was. He just had to trust that she had gotten safely out of the way in time. And was she worried about him? She had no idea where he or Bridget were.

"Mine's dead too," Dev said.

Matt felt himself getting antsy. He tapped his foot and drummed his fingers on the side of the boat. He chewed on his bottom lip.

He didn't know how much more of this he could take. What if they didn't find Bridget soon—or at all?

It seemed to Matt that this time, the problem was way, way bigger than the solution. In fact, it was the biggest problem Matt had ever encountered, and the plain truth was that he was scared.

What's the solution this time? Matt wanted to ask his dad.

Because Matt couldn't think of one.

The reality of their predicament threatened to flatten Matt. It was as if they had been dropped in the middle of a strange and never-ending sea with no navigation, no way to communicate, and no hope. He felt no closer to finding his sister now than he had the moment the water came crashing through their world.

Matt had never felt so hopeless in his life.

"We're going to find her," Dev said softly.

Matt didn't reply. He appreciated that Dev was just trying to help—but was it worse to hang on to false hope? What if they *weren't* going to find her? What if Bridget really wasn't okay?

No, Matt wasn't going to think that way.

"I'm really sorry I got you into this, Dev. You shouldn't be here."

Dev laughed. "You didn't start the flood. And no offense, but you couldn't do this on your own. Or at least, you shouldn't have to." His voice grew heavy. "No one should."

Through the haze of his despair, Matt felt a flash of gratitude. "Thanks," was all he managed to say. He returned his gaze to the sky. It was a bright blue compared to the murky green water. "Just do me a favor and don't get hurt?"

"I don't plan to."

Scout whimpered on the bow, and his head started flicking to and fro, like he was following a sound.

"What is it, Scout?" Matt and Dev said at the same time. Matt's heart instantly started pumping hard.

Scout stood up. His ears were locked forward and his tail pointed behind him. His nose twitched, and his eyes lit on one spot, then another. He sniffed at the air.

He whimpered again and set his eyes on a spot straight ahead.

"Dev, let's go!" Matt said, a note of urgency in his voice.

Dev sliced the paddle into the water and gave them a good push. They hit the current. The boat—and Matt's heart rate—sped up.

Scout's snout bobbed on the air. Every now and then, his ears swiveled backward or forward and he scratched lightly at the kayak's surface with his front paws, but he didn't sit, and he didn't give them the signal to stop.

Scout was acting strange—not like he had earlier

when he was tracking. Was he really following a scent, Matt wondered, or was he still out of it from his Dumpster encounter? Did dogs get concussions?

Matt wished he knew what Scout was thinking.

Suddenly, Scout dropped into a low crouch. Matt held out a hand to Dev, signaling at him to stop paddling. Dev froze with the paddle hanging in the air just above the surface of the water.

Was this it? Were they close to Bridget?

Matt scanned the surrounding area and the water below. He didn't see anything different—just endless water and floating debris. He listened carefully, straining to hear something—anything—in the silence. There was nothing.

The fur on Scout's back stood on end, and the fur on his tail bloomed into a bushy shape.

Something had spooked him.

Matt waited for the dog to either stand up or sit down, but he remained in his low crouch. And then suddenly Scout was rising up, pushing himself forward, his legs angling out behind him as he vaulted through the air and out, out, out into the water.

Scout had jumped off the kayak and landed in the water with a loud splash.

"Scout!" Matt yelled. But Scout was swimming hard. He knew where he wanted to go, and he was doing everything in his power to get there. "Come back!" Matt called. But there was no point. Scout was after something.

Scout moved purposefully through the water. But something was wrong. Matt watched in horror as Scout started to drift sideways, moving away from the direction in which he was trying to swim.

Matt felt the kayak sliding sideways too. He looked at Dev, but he wasn't paddling. Something else was happening.

Suddenly the kayak was sucked into some kind of flood channel—where the water churned and moved as swiftly as a raging river.

It looked like Scout had gotten caught in the current, and he couldn't fight it.

"Dev, paddle! Paddle toward him!"

Dev worked as hard as he could to catch up to Scout, but the kayak was caught in the same churning flow. They were all moving fast—too fast. The kayak was out of control. Dev tried to steer it, but to no avail.

Scout got tossed around in the water ahead of them.

He snorted water from his nose and kept pumping his legs.

Matt and Dev sped along closely behind him.

"Oh no—no—" Matt felt a wash of fear as he looked about thirty feet ahead. They were heading directly for a debris field that eddied in a wide circle. Tree limbs, shards of rock, massive clumps of wet leaves all spiraled around a center.

Scout hit it first. Matt saw a look of panic cross the dog's face as he got sucked into the circular motion. Scout fought against it, but he was helpless and too light compared to the mass of solid objects. A thick tree branch moving in the same direction—but much faster—swooped toward Scout, just barely missing him.

Matt gasped. If Scout got hit again . . .

He needed their help—fast.

"Dev," Matt cried. "What do we do? Can you get in there?"

"I'm trying," Dev grunted. He was paddling frantically. Finally, they caught the eddy too, but it was rough going, like a huge, dangerous whirlpool. The tip of the kayak's bow whacked into a large slab of plywood, spinning the craft unevenly and tipping it sharply onto its side. Matt and Dev clung to its smooth plastic surface, desperate to hang on. Matt felt the boat angling sharper and sharper, until they were on the verge of capsizing. Matt squeezed his eyes shut.

Then, as quickly as they had tipped over, they flopped back down right side up. Dev began to paddle again. Matt looked around desperately for Scout. He was still ahead of them in the swirl, and he still had his head above water—barely.

"Go, Dev!" Matt shouted.

"Almost there," Dev grunted back. And he did it: Dev managed to push them over and through, into the center of the spiral.

It was calmer there. They spun in a slow circle while the debris—and Scout—moved in a faster circle around them. Dev pushed them as close to Scout's trajectory as possible.

Matt reached out over the bow. So close.

"Closer," he said to Dev.

Dev paddled a little farther. He switched the paddle from one side of the kayak to the other, in a quick jabbing motion, trying to keep the craft as stable as possible. Matt leaned forward some more, stretching his arms. He teetered on the edge of falling in.

"Go!" Dev said. Matt lunged forward and wrapped

his hands around Scout's wet, slippery chest. Fear spiked through Matt as he started to fall into the water on top of Scout. Dev lurched forward and landed on top of Matt's legs.

Dev braced Matt while Matt held on tightly to Scout, pulling him in closer toward the kayak.

Matt pulled Scout into the boat.

Anger welled up in Matt's chest. After everything they'd been through that day—after the close calls and amazing saves—had he been wrong about Scout all this time? Was his mother right about Scout after all? "Darn it, Scout," Matt scolded him. "You have to listen—you can't just go rogue or you're going to get us all killed!"

Shaking and in shock, Scout curled up in a little ball by Matt's feet. He dropped his head down onto his back paws. He looked up at Matt, his eyes sadder than anything Matt had ever seen.

Matt exhaled loudly and flopped down in his seat, threw his head back, and closed his eyes.

The three of them sat silently for a long moment as the kayak spun in a tight circle and drifted in a larger one. But Matt and Dev didn't care where the boat was going right then. They just needed to catch their breath and count their lucky stars.

After a few minutes, Dev picked up the paddle and steered them back into the current. Once Matt could feel his limbs again, he sat up and looked down at Scout. Scout raised his head and held Matt's gaze.

Matt's mind was running wild. *I haven't found my sister, I have no idea if my mom is okay, and I just yelled at a dog—who's the best chance we have of getting out of this.*

He felt sick to his stomach for the way he had spoken to Scout.

And then an even worse realization washed over Matt: Everything he'd just shouted at Scout was advice Bridget and Dev had tried to give *him*.

Matt needed to listen just as much as Scout did. He thought back to all the dumb, rash decisions he'd made in the past week or so, and how many people he had put in jeopardy because of them. Matt felt horrible.

He owed them all an apology. If he got the chance to give it to them.

Matt needed to start with Scout. He leaned down and took Scout's head in his hands. He opened his mouth to say sorry, but before he could get the words out, Scout scrambled to his feet and began barking like crazy.

Matt and Dev nearly jumped out of their skin.

"Jeez, Scout!" Dev said.

"Scout, settle down," Matt said. Scout had stepped onto the bow again, and he was a changed dog. He was fixated on something—and determined to get to it. Scout's neck stretched forward and his head was down. His brown-and-white ears sat all the way forward on his head, while his tail curved up and out behind him like a fishing hook. He leaned down over the water, his nose hovering close to the surface. He raised his head again and stared into the distance.

And then Scout's tail started wagging so hard Matt could feel a breeze. He barked repeatedly, loudly.

Scout was . . . happy? He was communicating with someone only he could sense was nearby. Matt scanned the horizon, and his heart jumped into his throat when he saw a shape up ahead, in the center of the waterway. Matt could just make out the outlines of a car, submerged to the top of its windshield. The car was wedged in the crook of a toppled tree, and water rushed around it.

Sitting on top of it, holding on for dear life, was a familiar figure.

Bridget.

16

"HELP! PLEASE!"

It was the greatest sound ever. Bridget's voice.

Scout let out one loud bark, then sat down. He looked back at Matt, as if to say *I got us here. Now it's up to you.*

The kayak had slowed to a near standstill.

"Bridget!" Matt waved his arms in the air and screamed so loud his throat burned. "Bridget! We're here!"

"Matt? Is that you?!" She looked around frantically until she spotted him.

"It's me. Hang on—we'll get you."

"Hurry, Matt!" she replied.

"Let's go, Dev—paddle!" He pointed toward his

sister. Every nerve in Matt's body felt charged. He got to his knees in the kayak, fighting the urge to paddle with his hands to get them to her faster. The boat rocked under him.

"Careful, dude." Dev steadied the boat as best he could.

Reluctantly, Matt sat back down. Dev was right, but every second that ticked by felt like a minute, and the minutes felt like hours.

"It's slippery," Bridget cried. "I'm going to fall off!"

The fear in her voice was like a knife in Matt's heart. Scout must have heard it too. He barked and whimpered at the front of the kayak.

"Scout—easy." Matt soothed the dog. "We're coming right now," he called to Bridget. But they weren't. They were still just floating.

Dev squinted into the distance and pointed toward the car. "The water's moving really fast where she is. See that?"

Matt nodded.

"So," Dev went on, "we could go flying right past her. And we'd have to paddle back upstream."

Matt was silent, thinking, studying the current and the water level and the churn on the surface.

What would his dad do? What would his mom say to her troops in this situation?

They would say *Do what you're good at.*

If there was one thing Matt was good at, it was controlling a kayak. He could sense the ripples under the surface, the crosscurrents and gentle tugging around rocks and underwater surfaces. He could read the water—and he could make a kayak go where he wanted it to go.

"Matt, did you hear me?"

He nodded. He had a plan. "I got this." He held out his hand for the paddle, and Dev handed it to him. Matt dipped it into the water and steered the boat a few feet to the left, then a few feet back the other way, then upstream. He let the paddle hang in the water as they floated downstream. He studied the shape of the fast-flowing water around Bridget.

He was ready.

"Are you coming?" Bridget's voice was shrill with fear. "The water's getting higher."

"Don't worry—we're on our way."

She was quiet for a second. "This really isn't a good time to be late, Matt."

Matt laughed out loud and shook his head. "This really isn't a good time to be sarcastic, Bridge."

"Fine. Now please get over here."

"When we get there, climb onto the kayak fast, okay?"

"I don't know—it's so slippery. I'm scared to let go."

"It's only going to be scary for a second," Matt reassured her. "Not even a second! Like, a millisecond." He turned to Dev, who looked a little pale. "When we get to the car, you grab on to it—any part of it you can get your hands on, okay? I'll get her." Dev nodded. "You ready?"

"Sure." Dev didn't sound sure.

"On three. One. Two. Three."

Matt paddled them into the rush of water. They took off toward the car as if an unseen force propelled them from underneath. Matt moved fast, paddling on one side, then the other, and back, pointing them precisely where they needed to go.

They were twenty feet from the car.

They were ten feet from the car.

It happened in slow motion, but all at once. The car grew bigger and bigger until suddenly it was rushing right at them. Matt dropped the paddle to his lap. "Go!" he shouted at Dev. "Go go go go go!" he shouted at Bridget.

Everyone scrambled into motion at the exact same moment. Dev's hands shot out and grabbed the window frame of the car, halting their trajectory and pulling the kayak up against it. Bridget reached out her arms, flinging herself face-first toward the boat. Matt grabbed hold of Bridget's arms above the elbows. Scout jumped up and closed his teeth around Bridget's sleeve as she slid onto the kayak.

Dev was concentrating hard. His knuckles were turning white and shaking as he gripped the window, holding the full weight of their loaded boat against the current.

Bridget was almost entirely on top of the kayak, which sank lower under her weight but stayed afloat.

They had her.

And then they didn't.

At first Matt didn't understand what was happening. He felt the kayak rising as it suddenly became more buoyant. The boat was tilting toward the car. Scout was leaning sharply; no, he wasn't leaning, he was falling.

Bridget was sliding out of Matt's grip, slipping down . . . down . . . into the roiling gray water between the car and the kayak. Matt squeezed her arms so tightly he could see the marks where he cut off her circulation.

He leaned back for leverage, but she was too slippery. He couldn't hang on.

Her arms slipped through his hands and he caught her by the wrists. She was up to her chin in the water. Scout had landed on his side at the edge of the kayak.

Matt gritted his teeth. He gripped so hard he thought he would break her wrists, but he felt her fingers slide through his palms. He watched Bridget sink under the kayak. Then the water sped her away, and her scream receded as she moved out of reach.

She was gone.

Dev's face was frozen in shock. Matt couldn't find his voice. His hands tingled and twitched as if he were still holding on tightly to his sister, but they were empty.

"I can't hold on!" Dev said. He let go of the car and suddenly the kayak was sucked downstream—flipping over and spilling Matt, Dev, and Scout into the water.

The kayak was swept away. In the blink of an eye, their trusty vessel was gone.

Matt swirled along in the dark torrent. For a second, he didn't struggle against it. He gave in and closed his eyes. He felt like he was floating, weightless—he could have been orbiting the moon.

Matt opened his eyes. Bridget was nowhere to be

seen, but Dev and Scout were nearby. The three of them swam for their lives, but the flood pushed them this way and that. Water went up Matt's nose. His chin was just above the surface. The current swept them downstream until they slammed into something hard.

"Oof!" Matt grunted. It hurt, but he was relieved that something had stopped them.

Matt blinked water out of his eyes and saw that they were pressed up against the porch of a two-story house. He grabbed on to a beam and clung to it for dear life.

Scout dog-paddled beside him, struggling to keep his head above water. Matt pulled Scout in close. The dog relaxed in his arms, clearly exhausted. None of them would last much longer if they didn't get to higher ground.

Worst of all, Bridget was gone—again.

Matt forced himself to stay calm. If they could climb up onto the roof of the porch, they'd be safe— and he could look for his sister from up there.

"Head for the roof!" Matt tried to shout as water filled his mouth. Dev heard him and nodded. "Then I'll pass Scout up to you."

"Got it," Dev said, his mouth set in a grim line.

Dev pulled himself up on the porch beam and scaled

the side of the building. He grabbed at the wooden shingles, hauling himself up onto the roof.

"Okay, Scout," Matt said to the dog. "Get on my shoulders and Dev's gonna grab you."

Matt wasn't totally sure if Scout understood the command, but he let Matt hoist him up onto his shoulders. Scout was even heavier than normal, his fur matted down with water.

"Dev, grab him!"

"C'mon, Scout. Good boy," Dev said. He lay on his stomach and hung over the porch, reaching down to grab Scout under his front legs. He pulled Scout up and over the side. Then Dev helped Matt up too.

Dazed, Matt took a deep breath, feeling the cold water that had soaked into his clothes and the fresh air in his lungs. He took a minute to slow his heartbeat. Scout shook himself out, spraying water everywhere, then sat down, panting.

Matt gave Scout a scratch behind the ears, but he couldn't just sit there—he had to look for his sister. Matt staggered to his feet. He took one step, then gasped.

There, climbing up on the other side of the roof, was Bridget.

Matt's heart swelled with relief and joy.

17

BRIDGET STOOD WIPING WATER FROM HER FACE.

Matt walked over to her. The porch roof was squishy with all the liquid it had absorbed. Without a word, Bridget reached out and wrapped her arms around Matt, pulling him in for a hug. For once, Matt didn't roll his eyes. Instead, he hugged her right back.

"Thanks," she said into his shoulder.

"You're welcome. We should not tell Mom about this, right?"

"Probably not."

Scout wedged himself between them.

"Hi, Scout." Bridget patted his soggy head. "What are you doing here?" She gave Matt a questioning look.

"Um, it's a long story . . ." Matt said sheepishly.

"Hi." Dev waved at Bridget. "I'm Dev."

"Hi. Thanks for saving me."

"Anytime." Dev shrugged.

As they talked, Matt saw Scout's ears go up and move in different directions—one forward and one slightly back. That, Matt had come to recognize, was what Scout did when he noticed something was wrong. Matt looked around and tried to figure out the problem. It didn't take long: The water was still rising.

"Hey, guys, we have an issue," Matt said.

Dev and Bridget saw it too. They had just barely caught their breath, but they weren't safe yet.

"What do we do?" Dev asked.

"Let me think," Matt said.

"Well, you better think fast," Bridget said as the water began sloshing onto the roof. It quickly covered their toes. Scout picked a paw up out of the water and shook it.

Soon the water was up to Matt's shins.

Matt trudged a few feet away and looked up at the second floor of the house that had served as their landing pad. "We can get up there." He pointed at the second-story rooftop.

"Let's go." Dev reached up and grabbed the bottom corner of a window.

"Being tall is handy," Matt remarked.

"It can be." Dev grunted as he pulled himself up by his fingertips. "Being a rock climber doesn't hurt either." He got a knee up on the windowsill and pulled himself onto it. Then he swung himself up onto the higher roof. He lay on his stomach and reached down for Bridget. She grabbed his hands, and he helped her up.

"Scout—come!" Scout splashed over. Again, Matt picked him up under the armpits and held him up to Dev, who pulled him to safety. Matt climbed up last.

They sprawled out on the wet shingles, catching their breath. Every muscle in Matt's body was shaking. Side by side, they stared up at the sky, while Scout leaned into Matt.

"Matt?" Bridget said after a moment.

"Yeah?"

"If we survive this, I'm going to kill you."

"Fair enough." He fell quiet as he thought through their options. They needed to get off this roof before things got even worse, but they were surrounded by the racing floodwaters below and had no boat, no radio, and no food. Even if the phone lines were working, his phone was now totally waterlogged. They'd have to figure out another way to call for help.

"Bridge," Matt said.

"Yeah?"

"I have an idea."

Everyone got to work, following Matt's instructions. They peeled off their wet outer layers of clothing and arranged them into a message. Matt stood back to read their handiwork.

The letters SOS stood out from the roof in bright colors.

It felt good to take off all their wet and dirty clothes. Matt felt the hot sun drying the thin T-shirt on his back.

Scout nosed at a wet sock.

"Now what?" Bridget asked.

"Now I guess we wait?" Matt said.

They sat on the roof, hoping help would come quickly. There was nothing else they could do. Matt could feel exhaustion set into his bones. Scout lay next to him, his soft head in Matt's lap. Matt stroked Scout's ears.

Matt could tell that even though Scout was relaxed, he was still in work mode. Even when search-and-rescue dogs had found their subject, they were trained to wait with survivors and comfort them. And that's exactly what Scout was doing.

Because, Matt realized, they were all survivors.

All of a sudden, Scout's head shot up and he scanned the area watchfully. Matt looked around to see what Scout was sensing. Could it be more trouble?

"Look!" Bridget shouted. She pointed into the air at a far-off spot in the sky, just as Scout hopped to his feet and started barking.

Dev exhaled a sigh of relief. "Do I hear what I think I hear?"

"If you think you hear a helicopter, then yes!" Bridget said.

The beating sound of a rotor grew louder as the aircraft got closer. Matt felt the *thunk, thunk, thunk* vibration in his chest. Matt, Bridget, and Dev got to their feet and waved their hands in the air, while Scout ran in circles around their legs and howled up at the sky.

The helicopter hovered directly above them, blowing their hair around and kicking up water, spraying their faces.

The door to the aircraft opened, and a soldier in rescue gear stepped through it and quickly descended on a steel cable. She landed and shouted over the chopper blades.

"Matt? Bridget? Everybody all right?"

Matt and Bridget nodded in unison.

"We followed your trail from the grocery store to the library to here. We're going to get you out of here, kids. Just hang tight for me. Your mom is waiting for you."

Matt felt almost dizzy with relief that his mom was okay.

The soldier raised her hand to signal someone still in the helicopter. A large rescue basket dropped from the open door and floated down toward them. It plunked onto the wet roof.

The basket was rectangular, about knee-high, with four arms that extended upward to form a canopy. Two orange flotation devices dangled from its sides. Another steel cable was hooked to the top of the canopy. The cable extended straight up to the helicopter.

The soldier guided Bridget over to the basket and helped her step over the side and sit down. The woman gave a thumbs-up to the helicopter, and the basket began, slowly, to rise, spinning in a slow circle as it went.

Matt waved at Bridget, whose face was stricken with fear. She couldn't wave back—she was white-knuckling the metal bars so tightly that Matt thought she might bend them. He watched her go up and up, holding his breath as she twisted and turned in the sky. When the basket reached the helicopter, another soldier leaned out and pulled it into the cabin. After a moment, the basket reappeared and descended again.

Dev went up next. Then it was Matt's and Scout's turn. While they waited for the basket to come back down, Matt took a few steps over to the side of the roof. He looked down at the surging water below, still unable to believe that it was real.

Matt couldn't wait to see his mom—though now that he had a second to think about it, he realized he was going to have to confess to her that he had sprung Scout from the kennel.

Well, he figured, that was probably the least of his mom's worries at this point.

Out of nowhere, Matt's field of vision got wavy. Was the vibration of the helicopter blade shaking the whole house they stood on? Or were his legs just shaky?

The sensation got worse—but this time, Matt knew it wasn't the helicopter. This time, it was clearly the house itself that was shaking—hard. Matt looked over at Scout, but before he had time to react, the space between him and Scout opened up like a chasm. Suddenly, the whole side of the house simply fell away, out from under his feet. Part of the flooded first floor had collapsed, taking some of the roof down with it, and Matt was falling backward, straight down into the water below. He reached out but grabbed at air.

Just a couple of feet away, Scout was on safe ground. He stood on the edge of the crumbling roof, looking down at Matt and barking frantically.

Matt hit the water with a stinging splat. The last thing he saw before losing consciousness was Scout leaping from the roof, his legs splayed, sailing down toward the water.

He was coming to save Matt.

Matt was being dragged by the shoulder of his jacket. His arms and legs felt like they weighed a thousand pounds each, and he couldn't move them.

He opened his eyes, and the sky spun in big, wide swoops all around him. He closed his eyes again, willing the world to be steady.

He woke again to someone punching him in the chest. Or at least that's what it felt like. Now someone was scratching his face with something rough and bumpy . . . and wet.

Matt felt hot breath on his face. He opened one eye carefully and saw a blur of pink. He shut his eye quickly and let Scout lick his face some more. The dog had his front paws planted against Matt's chest and was desperately trying to wake him up.

The spinning had slowed, but Matt's stomach hurt—bad. He rolled to the side, tossing Scout off of him, and coughed up what seemed like a gallon of water. He took a few ragged breaths, wiped his face on his sleeve, and lay back again.

Scout sat down next to him and gave him one more lick on the cheek.

"Thanks, pal."

Matt's head was throbbing, but his mind was clearing. He rose up on his elbows to find himself lying on a dirt embankment. Water rushed around him. The soldier was unclipping herself from the helicopter cable that had lowered her to the ground nearby. She ran over and dropped to her knees at his side.

"Matt—are you okay—can you move?"

"I'm fine," he said. "Just sore."

"You're a lucky guy," the soldier said. "That dog saved your life. He jumped into the water right after you and pulled you out. If that current had gotten you while you were out cold . . ." She grimaced. "It would have been bad."

The rescue basket landed a few feet away.

The soldier helped Matt get up slowly and climb into it. Scout followed close on his heels and jumped in after him.

Scout lay down across Matt's legs, and Matt gave the soldier a thumbs-up.

They lifted off the ground and Matt and Scout rose past the house, past the roof, and into the sky. It had gotten late. The evening air brushed against Matt's skin, and the sunset cast a glow across the land. He could see clearly for miles. Water was everywhere. In the distance, his town was dark—the power hadn't come back on yet—but he could make out the tops of the office buildings downtown.

For the first time since the water had ravaged everything, Matt felt like things would be okay.

18

THE SOLDIER IN THE HELICOPTER HEAVED Matt out of the basket. Scout hopped out on his own, trotted to a corner, and lay down—as if nothing major had happened at all. Bridget and Dev were wrapped in metallic rescue blankets for warmth and strapped into seats against the wall.

Matt nodded and mouthed *Thank you* to his new friend. Dev saluted him and smiled.

The soldier wrapped Matt in a metallic blanket, handed him a water bottle, and gestured to him to drink. Matt took a long slug, letting the water wash through him.

They sent the basket down one last time for the

soldier on the ground. Matt buckled himself into the seat next to Dev. Scout got up, crossed to Matt, and put his front paws and head on Matt's lap. Matt tipped the water bottle to Scout's mouth, and the dog drained it.

Matt leaned down, wrapped his hands around Scout's neck, and rested his head on the dog's back. He felt the rise and fall of Scout's breathing. He stayed there while the soldier from the ground climbed aboard, and as the door slammed shut behind her.

As the helicopter rose, picked up speed, and tilted at a sharp angle, Matt buried his face in Scout's fur and closed his eyes.

"Good boy," Matt whispered into Scout's ear.

"Give me the remote."

"No."

"But you have terrible taste in television, Matt."

"If you don't like it, then leave."

"Ha." Bridget waved an arm around their hospital room, which was filled to the brim with flowers, trays of homemade brownies, and one large tan-and-white dog sprawled across Matt's legs, snoring loudly and twitching as he dreamed.

The door flew open and their mom sailed in carrying a pizza box.

"That smells so good!" Bridget said.

"Over here, Mom," Matt said. "I'm starving—the food here is the worst."

"Actually," Dev said from the doorway, "your mom promised me the first slice. Sorry, guys." He pulled his hospital gown tightly around himself and shuffled into the room in his fuzzy slippers. "My parents just left and I already finished all the food they brought."

Scout raised his head and sniffed at the scent of hot pizza. He dropped his head back down and was instantly asleep again.

Matt's mom handed out slices and took one for herself. "Dev," she mumbled through a mouthful, "you're going to get tired of hearing me say this, but thank you again for saving my kids."

"You're welcome, Mrs.—er, Colonel Tackett. Matt and Scout did all the hard work. I was just backup."

"Dev, you know I couldn't have done it without you," Matt said. He had inhaled his pizza. "And now you can help me out again by handing me another slice of pizza."

"That's what friends are for," Dev said, slapping a slice into Matt's palm.

"For real, guys." Matt's mom's eyes were dewy. "I'm so thankful you're safe. And I'm so proud of you for—"

She was cut off by the pillow that thwacked her on her arm.

"Mom!" Bridget cackled. "We know! You're proud! Stop it!"

"You're going to pay for that, dear daughter!" She laughed and picked up the pillow from the floor, tossing it back onto Bridget's bed.

"If I threw a pillow at my mom," Dev said to Bridget, "I'd be grounded."

As Dev passed a slice over to Bridget, Matt turned to his mom.

"Hey, Mom?" Matt said.

"Yeah, bud?"

"Can we stay here for a while? In Nevada?"

"I think maybe we can, Matt. Why?"

He looked over at Dev and Bridget laughing, then down at Scout, sleeping on his legs. He ran a hand through Scout's soft fur and looked out the window at the mountains rising in the distance. "I just want to. I like it here."

"Me too." She smiled at him. "I'll see what I can do to make that happen—for all of us." She paused. "That includes your dog."

"My dog, Scout?"

"Well, our dog, Scout." She pointed down at Scout, who had woken up at the sound of his name and was looking up at Matt adoringly. "This guy. You were right about him, Matt. He's clearly got what it takes. He just needed some time to know that for himself."

Matt thought about that for a moment. "Yeah." He nodded. "I guess that's exactly what he needed."

"In order to make Scout the best K-9 possible, I've decided that I'm going to train him personally," his mom said. "Which means he's going to live with us full-time. That okay with you?"

"That's awesome!" Matt pumped a fist in the air.

His mom's eyes got teary again. For once, Matt didn't get squirmy and try to change the subject. "Your dad will be so proud of you, Matt." She looked over at Bridget. "And you too, Bridge." Scout buried his nose in her hand.

Matt scratched Scout under the collar.

"You too, Scout," he said.

19

THE STREETS WERE STILL LINED WITH debris and fallen trees. Houses had their fronts ripped off. Cars lay on their sides.

But slowly, deliberately, the town was drying out and getting back on its feet. Matt's mom and her team were out there every day, hauling and hammering and rebuilding. Matt, Bridget, and Dev volunteered every morning to help people in town clean up their property and get their lives back on track.

Matt would never get used to the destruction, but he would do everything he could to help his town.

His town.

He rolled those words around in his mind as he

pedaled through the streets. This was his home now. For as long as he could remember, he'd never been able to say those words.

"Come on, Scout—let's hurry!" Matt pedaled harder, and Scout picked up speed at his side. Matt was huffing and puffing, but Scout—in his official National Guard K-9 Unit vest—was barely panting. He trotted along like running to Howler's Peak was just a warm-up for him.

Matt skidded to a stop at the base of the rock formation and laid his bike down on the ground.

A tall boy stood next to a tall woman who looked just like him. They were both in climbing gear.

"Hey, Dev. Hey, Gita."

"Hey, Matt," they said in unison.

"I'm so glad I could loan you my sister," Dev said, "especially since she already taught me everything I know about rock climbing."

"Well, that wouldn't take long." Gita gave an exaggerated eye roll.

"Cute," Dev said.

"Your sister is a great teacher," Matt piped in.

"Well, thanks, Matt," Gita said. "I'm glad someone around here appreciates me. But you're a great student—you've been working hard out here. You ready?"

"I'm ready."

"Let's do this. Get yourself suited up."

Matt stretched and shook out his arms and legs. He stuffed his feet into his climbing shoes, stepped into his harness, and clicked his helmet into place. He rubbed chalk on his hands and approached the hardest route Howler's had to offer.

Scout barked at Matt to get his attention. He skittered back and forth and stood up on his hind legs, keeping his eyes on Matt.

"Hey, Scout," Matt said. "Be right back."

Matt clipped in and began to climb while Gita coached him from below. Everything else fell away—the flood, school, waiting for his dad to come home, his mom working so hard, his sister . . . everything.

All he saw was the rock in front of him. All he felt was the rough surface under his fingertips and the crevice holding his foot steady. He heard the sound of his own breathing, and the call of a bird swooping in a wide circle far above him.

He made his way along steadily, building on each move, feeling for the right hold. It was a flawless climb.

Three-quarters of the way up, Matt heard a bark that brought a smile to his face. He looked down, and Scout was sitting between his mom and Bridget. But what were they doing here?

Standing right behind them was a familiar group. Dev, Amaiya, and the rest of his friends hooted and hollered at him.

"Matt! Matt! Matt!" they cheered.

Matt felt his face turn red, but he was glad they were there. "What's up, guys," he called down.

"You are," Dev shouted back. "Almost there, dude!"

Matt's mom gave him a little wave, and he smiled back. She held up her phone, and Matt could just make out his dad's face on the screen. Even he was there, watching Matt climb.

"Okay, Matt," Gita called up, "stay focused. Just keep doing what you're doing."

Matt turned back to the rock and took a couple of deep, steadying breaths. He ascended the last few feet and pulled himself over the top.

The shouts of joy from below echoed off the rocks and bounced around the desert floor. Finally, he'd climbed Howler's Peak.

"You did it!"

"That was sweet!"

"Dude—amazing!"

"Arrrrrooooooo!" Scout howled.

Matt couldn't help grinning to himself. He lay back on the warm rocks and let the sun hit his face while he caught his breath.

He heard his dad's voice in his head.

Know where you're going before you start. But remember that it will change along the way. Don't be afraid to reroute.

ACKNOWLEDGMENTS

We're no one without our people, and I'm so grateful for mine. Endless thanks to Les Morgenstein, Josh Bank, and Sara Shandler at Alloy; Margaret Anastas, Luana Horry, and the sales, marketing, and publicity groups at Harper; and Katelyn Hales at the Robin Straus Agency.

Romy Golan, they don't make a lot of them like you. Thanks for always being kind (and patient!).

Hayley Wagreich and Robin Straus, I'm out of dog metaphors, so I'll just say it: Thank you for everything. You are both exceptional, at your work and as humans.

I couldn't imagine life without our pup, Vida—who, I think, has wild dreams of daring rescues and close shaves. Thank you, Animal Lighthouse Rescue (alrcares.com), for your amazing efforts, and for filling so many homes with the kind of love only a dog can give.

And to my loyal, loving, and incredibly goofy pack—Brian, the goons, Virginia Wing, and Kunsang Bhuti. Thank you for your patience and constant support. You may now have the dining room table back. I love you all!